Selected Stories

Selected Stories

Rabindranath Tagore

GENERAL PRESS

Published by
GENERAL PRESS
4805/24, Fourth Floor, Krishna House
Ansari Road, Daryaganj, New Delhi - 110002
Ph : 011-23282971, 45795759
E-mail : generalpressindia@gmail.com

www.generalpress.in

© General Press

First Edition : 2018

ISBN : 9789387669307

Purchase our Books and eBooks online from:
Amazon.in | Flipkart.com | Infibeam.com

Published by Azeem Ahmad Khan for General Press

Contents

Rabindranath Tagore

Rabindranath Tagore (1861-1941) was the youngest son of Deben-dranath Tagore, a leader of the *Brahmo Samaj*, which was a new religious sect in nineteenth-century Bengal and which attempted a revival of the ultimate monistic basis of Hinduism as laid down in the *Upanishads*. He was educated at home; and although at seventeen he was sent to England for formal schooling, he did not finish his studies there. In his mature years, in addition to his many-sided literary activities, he managed the family estates, a project which brought him into close touch with common humanity and increased his interest in social reforms. He also started an experimental school at Shantiniketan where he tried his *Upanishadic* ideals of education. From time to time he participated in the Indian nationalist movement, though in his own non-sentimental and visionary way; and Gandhi, the political father of modern India, was his devoted friend. Tagore was knighted by the ruling British Government in 1915, but within a few years he resigned the honour as a protest against British policies in India.

Tagore had early success as a writer in his native Bengal. With his translations of some of his poems he became rapidly known in the West. In fact his fame attained a luminous height, taking him across continents on lecture tours and tours of friendship. For the world he became the voice of India's spiritual heritage; and for India, especially for Bengal, he became a great living institution.

Although Tagore wrote successfully in all literary genres, he was first of all a poet. Among his fifty and odd volumes of poetry are *Manasi* (1890)

{The Ideal One}, *Sonar Tari* (1894) {The Golden Boat}, *Gitan-jali* (1910) {Song Offerings}, *Gitimalya* (1914) {Wreath of Songs}, and *Balaka* (1916) {The Flight of Cranes}. The English renderings of his poetry, which include *The Gardener* (1913), *Fruit-Gather-ing* (1916), and *The Fugitive* (1921), do not generally correspond to particular volumes in the original Bengali; and in spite of its title, *Gitan-jali: Song Offerings* (1912), the most acclaimed of them, contains poems from other works besides its namesake. Tagore's major plays are *Raja* (1910) {*The King of the Dark Chamber*}, *Dakghar* (1912) {*The Post Office*}, *Achalayatan* (1912) {The Immovable}, *Muktadhara* (1922) {The Waterfall}, and *Raktakaravi* (1926) {*Red Oleanders*}. He is the author of several volumes of short stories and a number of novels, among them *Gora* (1910), *Ghare-Baire* (1916) {*The Home and the World*}, and *Yogayog* (1929) {*Crosscurrents*}. Besides these, he wrote musical dramas, dance dramas, essays of all types, travel diaries, and two autobiographies, one in his middle years and the other shortly before his death in 1941. Tagore also left numerous drawings and paintings, and songs for which he wrote the music himself.

1

The Cabuliwallah

My five-year old daughter Mini cannot live without chattering. I really believe that in all her life she has not wasted a minute in silence. Her mother is often vexed at this, and would like to stop her prattle, but I would not. For Mini to be quiet is unnatural, and I cannot bear it long. And so my own talk with her is always lively.

One morning, for instance, when I was in the midst of the seventeenth chapter of my new novel, my little Mini stole into the room, and putting her hand into mine, said: 'Father! Ramdayal, the doorkeeper, calls a crow a krow! He doesn't know anything, does he?'

Before I could explain to her the difference between one language and another in this world, she had embarked on the full tide of another subject. 'What do you think, Father? Bhola says there is an elephant in the clouds, blowing water out of his trunk, and that is why it rains!'

And then, darting off anew, while I sat still, trying to think of some reply to this: 'Father! What relation is Mother to you?'

With a grave face I contrived to say: 'Go and play with Bhola, Mini! I am busy!'

The window of my room overlooks the road. The child had seated herself at my feet near my table, and was playing softly, drumming on her knees. I was hard at work on my seventeenth chapter, in which Pratap Singh, the hero, has just caught Kanchanlata, the heroine, in his arms, and is about to escape with her by the third-storey window of the castle, when suddenly Mini left her play, and ran to the window, crying: 'A Cabuliwallah! A Cabuliwallah!' And indeed, in the street below, there was a Cabuliwallah, walking slowly along. He wore the loose, soiled clothing of his people, and a tall turban; he carried a bag on his back, and boxes of grapes in his hand.

I cannot tell what my daughter's feelings were when she saw this man, but she began to call him loudly. 'Ah!' thought I; 'he will come in, and my seventeenth chapter will never be finished!' At that very moment the Cabuliwallah turned, and looked up at the child. When she saw this, she was overcome by terror, and running to her mother's protection, disappeared. She had a blind belief that inside the bag, which the big man carried, there were perhaps two or three other children like herself. The pedlar meanwhile entered my doorway and greeted me with a smile.

So precarious was the position of my hero and my heroine, that my first impulse was to stop and buy something, since Mini had called the man to the house. I made some small purchases, and we began to talk about Abdur Rahman, the Russians, the English, and the Frontier Policy.

As he was about to leave, he asked: 'And where is the little girl, sir?'

And then, thinking that Mini must get rid of her false fear, I had her brought out.

She stood by my chair, and looked at the Cabuliwallah and his bag. He offered her nuts and raisins, but she would not be tempted, and only clung closer to me, with all her doubts increased.

This was their first meeting.

A few mornings later, however, as I was leaving the house, I was startled to find Mini, seated on a bench near the door, laughing and talking, with the great Cabuliwallah at her feet. In all her life, it appeared, my small daughter had never found so patient a listener, save her father. And already the corner of her little *sari* was stuffed with almonds and raisins, the gift of her visitor. 'Why did you give her those?' I said, and taking out an eight-anna piece, I handed it to him. The man accepted the money without demur, and put it into his pocket.

Alas, on my return, an hour later, I found the unfortunate coin had made twice its own worth of trouble! For the Cabuliwallah had given it to Mini; and her mother, catching sight of the bright round object, had pounced on the child with: 'Where did you get that eight-anna piece?'

'The Cabuliwallah gave it me,' said Mini cheerfully.

'The Cabuliwallah gave it you!' cried her mother greatly shocked. 'O Mini! How could you take it from him?'

I entered at that moment, and saving her from impending disaster, proceeded to make my own inquiries.

It was not the first or the second time, I found, that the two had met. The Cabuliwallah had overcome the child's first terror by a judicious bribe of nuts and almonds, and the two were now great friends.

They had many quaint jokes, which amused them greatly. Mini would seat herself before him, look down on his gigantic frame in all her tiny dignity, and with her face rippling with laughter would begin:

'O Cabuliwallah! Cabuliwallah! What have you got in your bag?'

And he would reply, in the nasal accents of the mountaineer: 'An elephant!' Not much cause for merriment, perhaps; but how they both enjoyed the fun! And for me, this child's talk with a grown-up man had always in it something strangely fascinating.

Then the Cabuliwallah, not to be behindhand would take his turn: 'Well, little one, and when are you going to your father-in-law's house?'

Now nearly every small Bengali maiden had heard long ago about her father-in-law's house; but we were a little new-fangled, and had kept these things from our child, so that Mini at this question must have been a trifle bewildered. But she would not show it, and with ready tact replied: 'Are *you* going there?'

Amongst men of the Cabuliwallah's class, however, it is well known that the words *father-in-law's house* have a double meaning. It is a euphemism for *jail*, the place where we are well cared for, at no expense to ourselves. In this sense would the sturdy pedlar take my daughter's question. 'Oh,' he would say, shaking his fist at an invisible policeman, 'I will thrash my father-in-law!' Hearing this, and picturing the poor discomfited relative, Mini would go off into peals of laughter in which her formidable friend would join.

These were autumn mornings, the very time of year when kings of old went forth to conquest; and I, without stirring from my little corner in Calcutta, would let my mind wander over the whole world. At the very name of another country, my heart would go out to it, and at the sight of a foreigner in the streets, I would fall to weaving a network of dreams—the mountains, the glens, and the forests of his distant land, with his cottage in their midst, and the free and independent life, or far away wilds. Perhaps scenes of travel are conjured up before me and pass and re-pass in my imagination all the more vividly, because I lead an existence so like a vegetable that a call to travel would fall upon me like a thunder-bolt. In the presence of this Cabuliwallah, I was immediately transported to the foot of arid mountain peaks, with narrow little defiles twisting in and out amongst their towering heights. I could see the string of camels bearing the merchandise, and the company of turbaned merchants, some carrying their queer old firearms, and some their spears, journeying downward towards the plains. I could see—. But at some such point Mini's mother would intervene, and implore me to 'beware of that man'.

Mini's mother is unfortunately very timid. Whenever she hears a noise in the streets, or sees people coming towards the house, she always jumps to the conclusion that they are either thieves, or drunkards, or snakes, or tigers, or malaria, or cockroaches, or caterpillars.

Even after all these years of experience, she is not able to overcome her terror. So she was full of doubts about the Cabuliwallah, and used to beg me to keep a watchful eye on him.

If I tried to laugh her fear gently away, she would turn round seriously, and ask me solemn questions:

Were children never kidnapped?

Was it not true that there was slavery in Cabul?

Was it so very absurd that this big man should be able to carry off a tiny child?

I urged that, though not impossible, it was very improbable. But this was not enough, and her dread persisted. But as it was a very vague dread, it did not seem right to forbid the man to the house, and the intimacy went on unchecked.

Once a year, in the middle of January, Rahman, the Cabuliwallah, used to return to his own country, and as the time approached, he would be very busy, going from house to house collecting his debts. This year, however, he could always find time to come and see Mini. It might have seemed to a stranger that there was some conspiracy between the two, for when he could not come in the morning, he would appear in the evening.

Even to me it was a little startling now and then, suddenly to surprise this tall, loose-garmented man laden with his bags, in the corner of a dark room; but when Mini ran in smiling, with her, 'O Cabuliwallah! Cabuliwallah!' and the two friends, so far apart in age, subsided into their old laughter and their old jokes, I felt reassured.

One morning, a few days before he had made up his mind to go, I was correcting proof-sheets in my study. The weather was chilly. Through the window the rays of the sun touched my feet, and the slight warmth was very welcome. It was nearly eight o'clock, and early pedestrians were returning home with their heads covered. Suddenly I heard an uproar in the street, and, looking out saw Rahman being led away bound between two policemen, and behind them a crowd of inquisitive boys. There were bloodstains on his clothes, and one of the policemen carried a knife. I hurried out, and stopping them, inquired what it all meant. Partly from one, partly from another, I gathered that a certain neighbour had owed the pedlar something for a Rampuri shawl, but had denied buying it, and that in the course of the quarrel Rahman had struck him. Now, in his excitement, the prisoner began calling his enemy all sorts of names, when suddenly in a verandah of my house appeared my little Mini, with her usual exclamation: 'O Cabuliwallah! Cabuliwallah!' Rahman's face lighted up as he turned to her. He had no bag under his arm today, so that she could not talk about the elephant with him. She therefore at once proceeded to the next question: 'Are you going to your father-in-law's house?' Rahman laughed and said: 'That is just where I am going, little one!' Then seeing that the reply did not amuse the child, he held up his fettered hands. 'Ah!' he said, 'I would have thrashed that old father-in-law, but my hands are bound!'

On a charge of murderous assault, Rahman was sentenced to several years' imprisonment.

Time passed, and he was forgotten. Our accustomed work in the accustomed place went on, and the thought of the once free mountaineer spending his years in prison seldom or never occurred to us. Even my light-hearted Mini, I am ashamed to say, forgot her old friend. New companions filled her life. As she grew older, she spent more of her time with girls. So much, indeed, did she spend with them that she came no more, as she used to do, to her father's room, so that I rarely had any opportunity of speaking to her.

Years had passed away. It was once more autumn, and we had made arrangements for our Mini's marriage. It was to take place during the Puja holidays. With Durga returning to Kailas, the light of our home also would depart to her husband's house, and leave her father's in shadow.

The morning was bright. After the rains, it seemed as though the air had been washed clean and the rays of the sun looked like pure gold. So bright were they, that they made even the sordid brick-walls of our Calcutta lanes radiant. Since early dawn the wedding-pipes had been sounding, and at each burst of sound my own heart throbbed.

The wail of the tune, *Bhairavi,* seemed to intensify the pain I felt at the approaching separation. My Mini was to be married that night.

From early morning noise and bustle had pervaded the house. In the courtyard there was the canopy to be slung on its bamboo poles; there were chandeliers with their tinkling sound to be hung in each room and verandah. There was endless hurry and excitement. I was sitting in my study, looking through the accounts, when someone entered, saluting respectfully, and stood before me. It was Rahman, the Cabuliwallah. At first I did not recognise him. He carried no bag, his long hair was cut short and his old vigour seemed to have gone. But he smiled, and I knew him again.

'When did you come, Rahman?' I asked him.

'Last evening,' he said, 'I was released from jail.'

The words struck harshly upon my ears. I had never before talked with one who had wounded his fellow-man, and my heart shrank within itself when I realised this; for I felt that the day would have been better-omened had he not appeared.

'There are ceremonies going on,' I said, 'and I am busy. Perhaps you could come another day?'

He immediately turned to go; but as he reached the door he hesitated, and said, 'May I not see the little one, sir, for a moment?' It was his belief that Mini was still the same. He had pictured her running to him as she used to do, calling 'O Cabuliwallah! Cabuliwallah!' He had imagined too that they would laugh and talk together, just as of old. Indeed, in memory of former days, he had brought, carefully wrapped up in a paper, a few almonds and raisins and grapes, obtained somehow or other from a countryman; for what little money had, had gone.

I repeated: 'There is a ceremony in the house, and you will not be able to see anyone today.'

The man's face fell. He looked wistfully at me for a moment, then said, 'Good morning,' and went out.

I felt a little sorry, and would have called him back, but I found he was returning of his own accord. He came close up to me and held out his offerings with the words: 'I have brought these few things, sir, for the little one. Will you give them to her?'

I took them, and was going to pay him, but he caught my hand and said: 'You are very kind, sir! Keep me in your memory. Do not offer me money! You have a little girl: I too have one like her in my own home. I think of her, and bring this fruit to your child—not to make a profit for myself.'

Saying this, he put his hand inside his big loose robe, and brought out a small and dirty piece of paper. Unfolding it with great care, he smoothed it out with both hands on my table. It bore the impression of a little hand. Not a photograph. Not a drawing. Merely the impression of an ink-smeared hand laid flat on the paper. This touch of the hand of his own little daughter he had carried always next to his heart, as he had come year after year to Calcutta to sell his wares in the streets.

Tears came to my eyes. I forgot that he was a poor Cabuli fruit-seller, while I was—. But no, what was I more than he? He also was a father.

That impression of the hand of his little Parvati in her distant mountain home reminded me of my own little Mini.

I sent for Mini immediately from the inner apartment. Many difficulties were raised, but I swept them aside. Clad in the red silk of her wedding-day, with the sandal paste on her forehead, and adorned as a young bride, Mini came and stood modestly before me.

The Cabuliwallah seemed amazed at the apparition. He could not revive their old friendship. At last he smiled and said: 'Little one, are you going to your father-in-law's house?'

But Mini now understood the meaning of the word 'father-in-law', and she could not answer him as of old. She blushed at the question, and stood before him with her bride-like face bowed down.

I remembered the day when the Cabuliwallah and my Mini had first met, and I felt sad. When she had gone, Rahman, sighed deeply and sat down on the floor. The idea had suddenly come to him that his daughter too must have grown up, while he had been away so long, and that he would have to make friends anew with her also. Assuredly he would not find her as she was when he left her. And besides, what might not have happened to her in these eight years?

The marriage-pipes sounded, and the mild autumn sunlight streamed round us. But Rahman sat in the little Calcutta lane, and saw before him the barren mountains of Afghanistan.

I took out a currency-note, gave it to him, and said: 'Go back to your daughter, Rahman, in your own country, and may the happiness of your meeting bring good fortune to my child!'

Having made this present, I had to curtail some of the festivities. I could not have the electric lights I had intended, nor the military band, and the ladies of the house were despondent about it. But to me the wedding-feast was all the more brighter for the thought that in a distant land a long-lost father had met again his only child.

2

The Postmaster

The postmaster took up his duties first in the village of Ulapur. Though the village was small, there was an indigo factory near it, and the proprietor, an Englishman, had managed to get a post office established.

Our postmaster belonged to Calcutta. He felt like a fish out of water in this remote village. His office and living-room were in a dark thatched shed, not far from a green, slimy pond, surrounded on all sides by a dense growth.

The man employed in the indigo factory had no leisure; moreover, they were hardly desirable companions for decent folk. Nor is a Calcutta boy an adept in the art of associating with others. Among strangers he appears either proud or ill at ease. At any rate, the postmaster had but little company; nor had he much work to do.

At times he tried his hand at writing verse. That the movement of the leaves and the clouds of the sky were enough to fill life with joy—such were the sentiments to which he sought to give expression. But God knows that the poor fellow would have felt it as the gift of a new life, if some genie of the *Arabian Nights* had in one night swept away the trees, leaves and all, and substituted for them a macadamised road, and had hidden the clouds from view with rows of tall houses.

The postmaster's salary was small. He had to cook his own meals, which he used to share with Ratan, an orphan girl of the village, who did odd jobs for him.

When in the evening, the smoke began to curl upwards from the village cow-sheds, and the cicadas chirped in every bush; when the mendicants of the Baul sect sang their shrill songs in their daily meeting place; when any poet, who had attempted to watch the movement of the leaves in the dense bamboo thickets, would have felt a ghostly shiver run down his back, the postmaster would light his little lamp, and call out 'Ratan.'

Ratan would sit outside, waiting for his call, and instead of coming in at once, would reply, 'Did you call me sir?'

'What are you doing?' the postmaster would ask.

'I must go and light the kitchen fire,' she would reply.

And the postmaster would say: 'Oh let the kitchen fire wait for a while; light me my pipe first.'

At last Ratan would enter, with puffed-out cheeks, vigorously blowing into a flame a live coal to light the tobacco. This would give the postmaster an opportunity of chatting with her. 'Well, Ratan,' perhaps he would begin, 'do you remember anything of your mother?' That was a fertile subject. Ratan partly remembered, and partly forgot. Her father had been fonder of her than her mother: him she recollected more vividly. He used to come home in the evening after his works, and one or two evenings stood out more clearly than others, like pictures in her memory. Ratan would sit on the floor near the postmaster's feet as memories crowded in upon her. She called to mind a little brother that she had—and how on some bygone cloudy day she had played at fishing with him on the edge of the pond, with a twig for a fishing-rod. Such little incidents would drive out greater events from her mind. Thus, as they talked, it would often get very late, and the postmaster would feel too lazy to do any cooking at all. Ratan would then hastily light the fire, and toast some unleavened bread, which, with the cold remnants of the morning meal, was enough for their supper.

On some evenings, seated at his desk in the corner of the big empty shed, the postmaster too would call up memories of his own home, of his mother and his sister, of those for whom in his exile his heart was sad—memories which were always haunting him, but which he could not reveal to the men of the factory, though he found himself naturally recalling them aloud in the presence of the simple little girl. And so it came about that the girl would allude to his people as mother, brother, and sister, as if she had known them all her life. Indeed, she had a complete picture of each one of them painted in her heart.

One day at noon, during a break in the rains, there was a cool soft breeze blowing; the smell of the damp grass and leaves in the hot sun felt like the warm breathing on one's body of the tired earth. A persistent bird repeated all the afternoon the burden of its one complaint in Nature's audience chamber.

The postmaster had nothing to do. The shimmer of freshly washed leaves, and the banked-up remnants of the retreating rain-clouds were sights to see; and the postmaster was watching them and thinking to himself: 'Oh, if only some kindred soul were near—just one loving human being whom I could hold near my heart!' This was exactly, he went on to think, what that bird was trying to say, and it was the same feeling which the murmuring leaves were striving to express. But no one knows, or would believe, that such an idea might also take possession of an ill-paid village postmaster in the deep, silent midday interval in his work.

The postmaster sighed, and called out 'Ratan.' Ratan was then stretched at full length beneath the guava-tree, busily engaged in eating unripe guavas. At the voice of her master, she ran up breathlessly, saying: 'Did you call me, Dada?' 'I was thinking of teaching you to read,' said the postmaster. And then for the rest of the afternoon he taught her the alphabet.

Thus, in a very short time, Ratan had got as far as the double consonants.

It seemed as though the rains would never end. Canals, ditches, and hollows were all flooded with water. Day and night the patter of rain was heard and the croaking of frogs. The village roads became impassable, and marketing had to be done in punts.

One heavily clouded morning, the postmaster's little pupil had been waiting for long outside the door to be called, but as the usual summons did not come, she took up her dogeared book, and slowly entered the room. She found her master lying on his bed, and thinking he was resting, she was about to retire on tiptoe, when she suddenly heard her name—'Ratan!' She turned at once and asked: 'Were you asleep, Dada?' The postmaster in a weak voice replied: 'I am not well. Feel my head; is it very hot?'

In the loneliness of his exile, and in the gloom of the rains, he needed a little tender nursing. He longed to call to mind the touch on his forehead of soft hands with tinkling bracelets, to imagine the presence of loving womanhood, the nearness of mother and sister. And the exile was not disappointed. Ratan ceased to be a little girl. She at once stepped into the post of mother, called in the village doctor, gave the patient his pills at the proper intervals, sat up all night by his pillow, cooked his gruel for him, and every now and then asked: 'Are you feeling a little better, Dada?'

It was some time before the postmaster, though still weak, was able to leave his sick-bed. 'No more of this,' said he with decision, 'I must apply for a transfer from this place.' He wrote off at once to Calcutta an application for a transfer, on the ground of the unhealthiness of the spot.

Relieved from her duties as nurse, Ratan again took up her former place outside the door. But she no longer heard the same old call. She would sometimes furtively peep inside to find the postmaster sitting on his chair, or stretched on his bed, and gazing absently into the air. While Ratan was awaiting her call, the postmaster was awaiting a reply to his application. The girl read her old lessons over and over again—her great fear was lest, when the call came, she might be found wanting in the double consonants. After a week's waiting, one evening her summons came. With an overflowing heart Ratan rushed into the room and cried, as she used to cry: 'Did you call me, Dada?'

The postmaster said: 'I am going away tomorrow, Ratan.'

'Where are you going, Dada?'

'I am going home.'

'When will you come back?'

'I am not coming back.'

Ratan asked no more. The postmaster, of his own accord, went on to tell her that his application for a transfer had been rejected, so he had resigned his post and was going home.

For a long time neither of them spoke. The lamp burned dimly, and from a leak in one corner of the thatch, water dripped steadily into an earthen vessel on the floor beneath.

After a while Ratan rose, and went off to the kitchen to prepare the meal; but she was not so quick about it as before. Many new things to think of had entered her little brain. When the postmaster had finished his supper, the girl suddenly asked him 'Dada, will you take me home with you?'

The postmaster laughed. 'What an idea!' said he. But he did not think it necessary to explain to the girl wherein lay the absurdity of such a course.

The whole night, awake and asleep, the postmaster's laughing reply haunted her—'What an idea!'

When he woke up in the morning, the postmaster found his bath ready. He had continued his Calcutta habit of bathing in water drawn and kept in pitchers, instead of taking a plunge in the river as was the custom of the village. For some reason or other, the girl could not ask him the time of his departure, she had therefore fetched the water from the river long before sunrise, so that it should be ready as soon as he might want it. After the bath came a call for Ratan. She entered without a sound, and looked silently into her master's face for orders. The master said: 'You need not be anxious about my going away, Ratan: I shall tell my successor to look after you.' These words were kindly meant, no doubt but inscrutable are the ways of a woman's heart!

Ratan had borne many a scolding from her master without complaint, but these kind words she could not bear. She burst out weeping, and said: 'No, no, you need not tell anybody anything at all about me; I don't want to stay here any longer.'

The postmaster was dumbfounded. He had never seen Ratan like this before.

The new man duly arrived, and the postmaster gave over charge, and prepared to depart. Just before starting he called Ratan and said: 'Here is something for you: I hope it will keep you for some little time.' He brought out from his pocket the whole of his month's salary, retaining only a trifle for the journey. Then Ratan fell at this feet and cried: 'O, Dada pray don't give me anything, don't in any way trouble about me,' and then she ran away out of sight.

The postmaster heaved a sigh, took up his bag, put his umbrella over his shoulder, and, accompanied by a man carrying his many-coloured tin trunk, slowly made for the boat.

When he got in and the boat was under way, and the rain-swollen river, like a stream of tears welling up from the earth, swirled and sobbed at her bows, then he felt grieved at heart; the sorrow-stricken face of a village girl seemed to represent for him the great unspoken pervading grief of Mother Earth herself. At one moment he felt an impulse to go back and bring away with him that lonely waif, forsaken of the world. But the wind had just filled the sails, the boat had got well into the middle of the turbulent current, and already the village was left behind, and its outlying burning-ground had come into sight.

So the traveller, borne on the breast of the swift-flowing river, consoled himself with philosophical reflections on the numberless meetings and partings in the world, and on death, the great parting, from which there is no return.

But Ratan had no philosophy. She was wandering about the post office with the tears streaming from her eyes. It may be that she had still a hope lurking in some corner of her heart that her Dada would return, and perhaps that is why she could not tear herself away. Alas, for our foolish human nature! Its fond mistakes are persistent. The dictates of reason take a long time to assert their sway.

The surest proofs meanwhile are disbelieved. One clings desperately to some vain hope, till a day comes when it has sucked the heart dry and then it breaks through its bonds and departs. After that comes the misery of awakening, and then once again the longing to get back into the maze of the same mistakes.

3

The Child's Return

$\mathcal{R}$aicharan was twelve years old when he came as a servant to his master's house. He belonged to the same caste as his master and was given his master's little son to nurse. As time went on, the boy left Raicharan's arms to go to school. From school he went to college, and after college he entered the judicial service. Until the time of the boy's marriage, Raicharan was his sole attendant.

But when a mistress came into the house, Raicharan found that he had two masters instead of one. All his former influence passed to the new mistress. This was compensated for by a fresh arrival. Anukul had a son born to him and Raicharan by his unsparing attentions soon obtained complete hold over the child. He would toss him up in his arms, call to him in absurd baby language, put his face close to the baby's and withdraw it again with a laugh.

Presently the child was able to crawl and venture outside the house. When Raicharan went to catch him, he would scream with mischievous laughter and try to evade him. Raicharan was amazed at the profound skill and exact judgement the baby showed when pursued. He would say to his mistress with a look of awe and mystery: 'You son will be a judge some day.'

New wonders came in their turn. It was to Raicharan an epoch in human history when the baby began to toddle. When he called his father Ba-ba and his mother Ma-ma and Raicharan Chan-na, then Raicharan's joy was boundless. He wanted to let the whole world know.

After a while Raicharan was asked to show his ingenuity in other ways. He had, for instance, to play the part of a horse, holding the reins between his teeth, and prancing with his feet. He had also to wrestle with his little charge; and if he could not, by a wrestler's trick, fall on his back defeated at the end, a great outcry was certain.

About this time Anukul was transferred to a district on the banks of the Padma. On his way through Calcutta, he bought his son a little go-cart, and at the same time a yellow satin waist-coat, a gold-laced cap, and gold bracelets and anklets. Raicharan loved to take this finery out and put it on his little charge whenever they went for a walk, and this he did with great pride and ceremony.

Then came the rainy season, and day after day the rain poured down. The hungry river, like an enormous serpent, swallowed terraces, villages, and cornfields, covering with its flood the tall grasses and wild casuarinas on the sandbanks. From time to time there was a deep thud as the river-banks crumbled. The unceasing roar of the main current could be heard from far away. Masses of foam, carried swiftly past, proved to the eye the swiftness of the stream.

One afternoon the rain stopped. It was cloudy, but cool and bright. Raicharan's little despot did not want to stay indoors on such a fine afternoon. His lordship climbed into the go-cart. Raicharan, between the shafts, dragged him slowly along till he reached the rice-fields on the banks of the river. There was no one in the fields, and no boat on the steam. Across the water, on the farther side, the clouds were rifted in the west. The silent ceremonial of the setting sun was revealed in all its glowing splendour. In the midst of that stillness, the child suddenly pointed in front of him and cried—'Chan-na! Pitty fow.'

On a mud-flat closeby stood a large *Kadamba* tree in full flower. My lord the baby looked at it with greedy eyes, and Raicharan knew immediately what he wanted. Only a short time before he had made, out of the flower-balls of this tree, a small go-cart and the child had been so happy dragging it about by a string, that for the whole day Raicharan was not asked to put on the reins at all. He was promoted from being a horse to being a groom.

But Raicharan had no wish that evening to go splashing knee-deep through the mud to reach the flowers. So he quickly pointed in the opposite direction, and cried: 'Look, baby look! Look at the bird!' And with all sorts of curious noises he pushed the go-cart rapidly away from the tree.

But a child, destined to be a judge, cannot be put off so easily. And besides, there was at the time nothing to attract his eyes. And you cannot keep up for ever the pretence of an imaginary bird.

The little Master's mind was made up, and Raicharan was at his wit's end. 'Very well, baby,' he said at last, 'you sit still in the cart, and I'll go and get you the pretty flower. Only mind you, don't go near the water.'

As he said this, he bared his legs to the knee, and waded through the oozing mud towards the tree.

The moment Raicharan had gone, his little Master's thoughts raced off to the forbidden water. The baby saw the river rushing by, splashing and gurgling as it went. It seemed as though the disobedient wavelets themselves were running away from some greater Raicharan with the laughter of a thousand children. At the sight of their mischievous sport, the heart of the human child grew excited and restless. He got down stealthily from the go-cart and toddled off towards the river. On his way he picked up a small stick and leant over the bank of the stream, pretending to fish. The mischievous fairies of the river with their mysterious voices seemed to be inviting him to enter their play-house.

Raicharan had plucked a handful of flowers from the tree and was carrying them back in a fold of his cloth, his face wreathed in smiles. But when he reached the go-cart, it was empty. He looked round on all sides, but there was no one there. He looked back at the cart, and there was no one there.

In that first terrible moment, his blood froze within him. Before his eyes the whole universe swam round like a dark mist. From the depths of his broken heart he gave one piercing cry: 'Master, Master, little Master!'

But no voice answered, 'Chan-na.' No child laughed mischievously back: no scream of baby delight welcomed his return. Only the river ran on with its splashing, gurgling noise as before, as though it knew nothing at all, and had no time to attend to such a tiny human event as the death of a child.

As the evening crept on, Raicharan's mistress became more and more anxious. She sent men out everywhere to search. They went with lanterns in their hands and reached at last the banks of the Padma. There they found Raicharan rushing up and down the fields, like a stormy wind, shouting in a voice of despair: 'Master, Master, little Master!'

When they got Raicharan home at last, he fell prostrate at the feet of his mistress. They shook him, and questioned him, and asked him repeatedly where he had left the child: but all he could say was that he knew nothing.

Though everyone held the opinion that the Padma had swallowed the child, there was still a lurking doubt left. For a band of gipsies had been noticed outside the village that afternoon, and some suspicion rested on them. The mother went so far in her wild grief as to think it possible that Raicharan himself had stolen the child. She called him aside with piteous entreaty and said: 'Raicharan, give me back my baby. Give me back my child. Take from me any money you want, but give me back my child!'

Raicharan only beat his forehead in reply. His mistress in her anger ordered him out of the house.

Anukul tried to reason his wife out of this wholly unjust suspicion: 'Why on earth', he said, 'should he commit such a crime as that?'

The mother only replied: 'The baby was wearing gold ornaments. Who knows?'

It was impossible to reason with her after that.

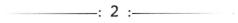

: 2 :

Raicharan went back to the village of his birth. He had no son, and there was no hope that a child would now be born to him. But it came about before the end of a year that his wife gave birth to a son and died.

An overwhelming resentment at first grew up in Raicharan's heart at the sight of this new baby. At the back of his mind was an indignant suspicion that it had come as an usurper in place of the little Master. He also thought that it would be a grave offence to be happy with a son of his own after what had happened to his master's little child. Indeed, if it had not been for a widowed sister, who mothered the new baby, it would not have lived long.

But gradually a change came over Raicharan's mind. A wonderful thing happened. This new baby in turn began to crawl about, and venture outside the house, bent on mischief. It also showed an amusing cleverness in making its escape to safety. Its voice, its laughter and tears, its gestures, were those of the little Master. Sometimes, when Raicharan listened to its crying, his heart suddenly began thumping wildly against his ribs, and it seemed to him that his former little Master was crying somewhere in the unknown land of death because he had lost his Chan-na.

Phailna (for that was the name Raicharan's sister gave to the new baby) soon began to talk. It learnt to say Ba-ba and Ma-ma with a baby accent. When Raicharan heard those familiar sounds, the mystery suddenly became clear. The little Master could not cast off the spell of his Chan-na and therefore he had been reborn in his house.

The three arguments in favour of this were, to Raicharan, altogether beyond dispute:

The new baby was born soon after his little Master's death.

His wife could never have accumulated such merit as to give birth to a son in middle age.

The new baby walked with toddling steps and called out Ba-ba and Ma-ma. There was no sign lacking—this was certainly the future judge.

Then suddenly Raicharan remembered that terrible accusation of the mother. 'Ah,' he said to himself in amazement, 'the mother's heart was right. She knew I had stolen her child.'

When once he had come to this conclusion, he was filled with remorse for his past neglect. He now gave himself over, body and soul, to the new baby and became its devoted attendant. He began to bring it up as if it were the son of a rich man. He bought a go-cart, a yellow satin waist-coat, and a gold-embroidered cap. He melted down the ornaments of his dead wife and made gold bangles and anklets. He refused to let the little one play with any child in the neighbourhood and became himself its sole companion day and night. As the baby grew to boyhood, he was so petted and spoilt and clad in such finery that the village children would call him 'Your Lordship', and jeer at him; and older people regarded Raicharan as unaccountably crazy about the child.

At last the time came for the boy to go to school. Raicharan sold his small piece of land and went to Calcutta. There with great difficulty he found employment as a servant and sent Phailna to school. He spared no pains to give him the best education, the best clothes, the best food. Meanwhile, he himself lived on a mere handful of rice and would say in secret: 'Ah, my little Master, my dear little Master, you loved me so much that you came back to my house. You will never suffer from any neglect of mine.'

In this way twelve years passed away. The boy could now read and write well. He was bright, good-looking, and in perfect health. He paid a great deal of attention to his personal appearance and took great care in the parting of his hair. He was inclined to extravagance, and spent money freely in finery and enjoyment. He could never quite regard Raicharan as a father because, though he had the affection of a father, his manner was that of a servant. A further fault was this, that Raicharan kept secret from everyone the fact that he himself was the father of the child.

The students of the hostel in which Phailna was a boarder, were greatly amused by Raicharan's country-manners, and I am afraid that behind his father's back, Phailna joined in their fun. But, in the bottom of their hearts, all the students loved the innocent and tender-hearted old man, and Phailna also was very fond of him. But, as I have said before, he loved him with a kind condescension.

As Raicharan grew older and older, his employer was continually finding fault with him for his incompetence. He starved himself for the boy's sake, so that he grew weaker in body and was no longer up to his daily task. He began to forget things and became dull and stupid. But his employer expected the work of a fully capable servant, and would listen to no excuse. The money that Raicharan had brought with him from the sale of his land was now exhausted and the boy continually grumbled about the state of his clothes and continually asked for more money.

———: **3** :———

At last Raicharan made up his mind. He threw up his work as a servant, and left some money with Phailna. Before leaving, he promised Phailna that after seeing to some necessary business in his native village, he would immediately return.

He went off at once to Baraset where Anukul was magistrate. Anukul's wife was still broken down with grief for she had no other child.

One evening Anukul was resting after a long and weary day in court. His wife was buying from a mendicant quack at an exorbitant price, a herb which, so the quack assured her, would ensure the birth of a child. Suddenly, in the courtyard, Anukul heard a voice raised in greeting, and he went out to see who was there. There before him stood Raicharan, and when he saw his old servant, Anukul's heart was softened. He asked him many questions, and offered to take him back into his employ.

But Raicharan only smiled faintly and said in reply: 'I merely want to make obeisance to my mistress.'

Anukul accompanied Raicharan into the house, but the mistress did not receive him as warmly as his old master had done. Raicharan took no notice, but with his hand clasped in appeal, said: 'It was not the Padma that stole your baby. It was I.'

'Great God!' Anukul exclaimed: 'What! Where is he?'

Raicharan replied: 'He is with me. I will bring him the day after tomorrow.'

It was Sunday, and so the magistrate's court was not sitting. From early morning both husband and wife were gazing expectantly along the road, waiting for Raicharan's appearance. At ten o'clock he came, leading Phailna by the hand.

Anukul's wife, without questioning his identity, took the boy on her lap and was wild with excitement, laughing, weeping, touching him, kissing his hair, and his forehead, and gazing into his face with hungry, eager eyes. The boy was very good-looking and was dressed like a gentleman's son. The heart of Anukul brimmed over with a sudden gush of affection.

Nevertheless the magistrate in him asked: 'Have you any proofs that he is my son?'

Raicharan said: 'Proof? How could there be any proof of such a deed? God alone knows that I and no one else in the world stole your boy.'

When Anukul saw how eagerly his wife clung to the boy, he realised how futile it was to ask for proofs. It would be wiser to believe.

And then—where could an old man like Raicharan get such a boy? And why should his faithful servant deceive him? He could surely hope for no gain from such deceit!

Still, he could not forget his old servant's lapse from duty, so he exclaimed: 'Raicharan, you must not remain any longer here.'

'Where shall I go, Master?' said Raicharan, in a voice choking with grief. Then with hands clasped imploringly, he added: 'I am old. Who will take an old man as a servant?'

The mistress said: 'Let him stay. My child will be pleased, and I forgive him.'

But Anukul's magisterial conscience would not let him permit this. 'No,' he said, 'he cannot be forgiven for what he has done.'

Raicharan bowed to the ground and clasped Anukul's feet. 'Master,' he cried, 'let me stay. It was not I that did it. It was God.'

Anukul's conscience was more shocked than ever when Raicharan tried to put the blame on God.

'No,' he said, 'I cannot allow it. I can trust you no longer. You have acted treacherously.'

Raicharan rose to his feet and said: 'It was not I that did it.'

'Who was it then?' asked Anukul.

Raicharan replied: 'It was my fate.'

But no educated man could take this for an excuse, and Anukul remained obdurate.

When Phailna saw that he was the wealthy magistrate's son, and not Raicharan's, he was at first angry, for the thought that he had been cheated all this time of his birthright. But seeing Raicharan in distress, he generously said to his father: 'Father, forgive him. Even if you don't let him live with us, let him at least have a small monthly pension.'

On hearing this, Raicharan was speechless. He looked for the last time on the face of his son. He made obeisance to his old master and mistress. Then he went out and mingled with the numberless people of the world.

At the end of the month Anukul sent some money to his village. But the money came back, for no person of the name of Raicharan could be found there.

4

The Home-Coming

Phatik Chakravarti was the ringleader among the boys of the village. One day a plan for new mischief entered his head. There was a heavy log lying on the mud-flat of the river, waiting to be shaped into a mast for a boat. His plan was that they should all work together to shift the log by main force from its place and roll it away. The owner of the log would be angry and surprised, while they would all enjoy the fun. Everyone supported the proposal, and it was carried unanimously.

But just as the fun was about to begin, Makhan, Phatik's young brother, sauntered up without a word and sat down on the log in front of them all. The boys were puzzled for a moment. One of them pushed him rather timidly, and told him to get up; but he remained quite unconcerned. He appeared like a young philosopher meditating on the futility of games. Phatik was furious. 'Makhan,' he cried, 'if you don't get up this minute, I'll thrash you!'

Makhan only moved to a more comfortable position.

Now, if Phatik was to keep his real dignity before the public, it was clear that he must carry out his threat. But his courage failed him at the crisis. His fertile brain, however, rapidly seized upon a new manoeuvre which would discomfort his brother and afford his followers added amusement. He gave the word of command to roll the log and Makhan over together. Makhan heard the order and made it a point of honour to stick on. But like those who attempt earthly fame in other matters, he over-looked the fact that there was peril in it.

The boys began to heave at the log with all their might, calling out, 'One, two, three, go!' At the word 'go' the log went; and with it went Makhan's philosophy, glory and all.

The other boys shouted themselves hoarse with delight. But Phatik was a little frightened. He knew what was coming. And he was not mistaken, for Makhan rose from Mother Earth blind as Fate and screaming like the Furies. He rushed at Phatik, scratched his face, beat him and kicked him, and then went crying home. The first act of the drama was over.

Phatik wiped his face, and sitting down on the edge of a sunken barge by the river-bank, began to nibble a piece of grass. A boat came up to the landing and a middle-aged man, with grey hair and dark moustache, stepped on shore. He saw the boy sitting there, doing nothing and asked him where the Chakravartis lived. Phatik went on nibbling the grass and said: 'Over there;' but it was quite impossible to tell where he pointed. The stranger asked him again. He swung his legs to and fro on the side of the barge and said: 'Go and find out,' and continued to nibble the grass.

But, at that moment, a servant came down from the house and told Phatik that his mother wanted him. Phatik refused to move. But on this occasion the servant was the master. He roughly took Phatik up and carried him, kicking and struggling in impotent rage.

When Phatik entered the house, his mother saw him and called out angrily: 'So you have been hitting Makhan again?'

Phatik answered indignantly: 'No, I haven't! Who told you that I had?'

His mother shouted: 'Don't tell lies! You have.'

Phatik said sullenly: 'I tell you, I haven't. You ask Makhan!' But Makhan thought it best to stick to his previous statement. He said: 'Yes, mother, Phatik did hit me.'

Phatik's patience was already exhausted. He could not bear this injustice. He rushed at Makhan and rained on him a shower of blows: 'Take that,' he cried, 'and that, and that, for telling lies.'

His mother took Makhan's side in a moment, and pulled Phatik away, returning his blows with equal vigour. When Phatik pushed her aside, she shouted out: 'What! You little villain! Would you hit your own mother?'

It was jut at this critical moment that the grey-haired stranger arrived. He asked what had occurred. Phatik looked sheepish and ashamed.

But when his mother stepped back and looked at the stranger, her anger was changed into surprise. For she recognised her brother and cried: 'Why, Dada! Where have you come from?'

As she said these words, she bowed to the ground and touched his feet. Her brother Bishambar had gone away soon after she had married, and had started business in Bombay. She herself had lost her husband while he was there. Bishambar had now come back to Calcutta, and had at once made inquiries concerning his sister. As soon as he found out where she was, he had hastened to see her.

The next few days were full of rejoicing. The brother asked how the two boys were being brought up. He was told by his sister that Phatik was a perpetual nuisance. He was lazy, disobedient, and wild. But Makhan was as good as gold, as quiet as a lamb, and very fond of reading. Bishambar kindly offered to take Phatik off his sister's hands and educate him with his own children in Calcutta. The widowed mother readily agreed. When his uncle asked Phatik if he would like to go to Calcutta with him, his joy knew no bounds, and he said: 'Oh, yes, yes, uncle!' in a way that made it quite clear that he meant it.

It was an immense relief to the mother to get rid of Phatik. She had a prejudice against the boy, and no love was lost between the two brothers.

She was in daily fear that he would some day either drown Makhan in the river, or break his head in a fight, or urge him on into some danger. At the same time she was a little distressed to see Phatik's extreme eagerness to leave his home.

Phatik, as soon as all was settled, kept asking his uncle every minute when they were to start. He was on pins all day long with excitement and lay awake most of the night. He bequeathed to Makhan, in perpetuity, his fishing-rod, his big knife, and his marbles. Indeed, at this time of departure, his generosity towards Makhan was unbounded.

When they reached Calcutta, Phatik met his aunt for the first time. She was by no means pleased with this unnecessary addition to her family. She found her own three boys quite enough to manage without taking anyone else. And to bring a village lad of fourteen into their midst was terribly upsetting. Bishambar should really have thought twice before committing such an indiscretion.

In this world there is no worse nuisance than a boy at the age of fourteen. He is neither ornamental nor useful. It is impossible to shower affection on him as on a smaller boy; and he is always getting in the way. If he talks with a childish lisp he is called a baby, and if in a grownup way he is called impertinent. In fact, talk of any kind from him is resented. Then he is at the unattractive, growing age. He grows out of his clothes with indecent haste; his voice grows hoarse and breaks and quavers; his face grows suddenly angular and unsightly. It is easy to excuse the shortcomings of early childhood, but it is hard to tolerate even unavoidable lapses in a boy of fourteen. He becomes painfully self-conscious, and when he talks with elderly people he is either unduly forward, or else so unduly shy that he appears ashamed of his own existence.

Yes, it is at this age that in his heart of hearts, a young lad most craves recognition and love and he becomes the devoted slave of anyone who shows him consideration. But none dare openly love him, for that would be regarded as undue indulgence and therefore bad for the boy. So, what with scolding and chiding, he becomes very much like a stray dog that has lost its master.

His own home is the only paradise that a boy of fourteen can know. To live in a strange house with strange people is little short of torture; while it is the height of bliss to receive the kind looks of women and never to suffer their slights.

It was anguish to Phatik to be an unwelcome guest in his aunt's house, constantly despised and slighted by this elderly woman. If she ever asked him to do anything for her, he would be so overjoyed that his joy would seem exaggerated; and then she would tell him not to be so stupid, but to get on with his lessons.

This constant neglect gave Phatik a feeling of almost physical oppression. He wanted to go out into the open country and fill his lungs with fresh air. But there was no open country to go to. Surrounded on all sides by Calcutta houses and walls, he would dream night after night of his village home and long to be back there. He remembered the glorious meadow where he used to fly his kite all day long; the broad river-banks where he would wander the livelong day, singing and shouting for joy; the narrow brooks where he could dive and swim whenever he liked. He thought of the band of boy companions over whom he was despot; and, above all, thoughts of even that tyrant mother of his, who had such a prejudice against him, filled his mind day and night. A kind of physical love like that of animals, a longing to be in the presence of the loved one, an inexpressible wistfulness during absence, a silent cry of the inmost heart for the mother, like the lowing of a calf in the twilight—this love, which was almost an animal instinct, stirred the heart of this shy, nervous, thin, uncouth and ugly boy. No one could understand it, but it preyed upon his mind continually.

There was no more backward boy in the whole school than Phatik. He gaped and remained silent when the teacher asked him a question, and like an overladen ass patiently suffered the many thrashings that were meted out to him. When other boys were out at play, he stood wistfully by the window and gazed at the roofs of the distant houses. And if by chance he espied children playing on the open terrace of a roof, his heart would ache with longing.

One day he summoned up all his courage and asked his uncle: 'Uncle, when can I go home?'

His uncle answered: 'Wait till the holidays come.'

But the holidays would not come till October and there was still a long time to wait.

One day Phatik lost his lesson book. Even with the help of books he had found it very difficult to prepare his lesson. But, now, it became impossible. Day after day the teacher caned him unmercifully. He became so abjectly miserable that even his cousins were ashamed to own him. They began to jeer and insult him more than even the other boys did. At last he went to his aunt and told her that he had lost his book.

With an expression of the greatest contempt she burst out: 'You great, clumsy, country lout! How can I afford to buy you new books five times a month, when I have my own family to look after?'

That night, on his way back from school, Phatik had a bad headache and a shivering-fit. He felt that he was going to have an attack of malaria. His one great fear was that he might be a nuisance to his aunt.

The next morning Phatik was nowhere to be seen. Search in the neighbourhood proved futile. The rain had been pouring in torrents all night, and those who went out to look for the boy were drenched to the skin. At last Bishambar asked the police to help him.

At nightfall a police van stopped at the door of the house. It was still raining and the streets were flooded. Two constables carried Phatik out in their arms and placed him before Bishambar. He was wet through from head to foot, covered with mud, while his face and eyes were flushed with fever and his limbs were trembling. Bishambar carried him in his arms and took him inside the house. When his wife saw him she exclaimed: 'What a heap of trouble this boy has given us! Hadn't you better send him home?'

Phatik heard her words and sobbed aloud: 'Uncle, I was just going home; but they dragged me back again.'

The fever rapidly increased, and throughout the night the boy was delirious. Bishambar brought in a doctor. Phatik opened his eyes, and looking up to the ceiling said vacantly: 'Uncle, have the holidays come yet?'

Bishambar wiped the tears from his eyes and took Phatik's thin burning hands in his own and sat by his side through the night. Again the boy began to mutter, till at last his voice rose almost to a shriek: 'Mother!' he cried, 'don't beat me like that......Mother! I *am* telling the truth!'

The next day Phatik for a short time became conscious. His eyes wandered round the room, as if he expected someone to come. At last, with an air of disappointment, his head sank back on the pillow.

With a deep sigh he turned his face to the wall.

Bishambar read his thoughts, and bending down his head, whispered: 'Phatik, I have sent for your mother.'

The day dragged on. The doctor said in a troubled voice that the boy's condition was very critical.

Phatik began to cry out: 'By the mark—three fathoms. By the mark—four fathoms. By the mark—' Many times had he heard the sailors on the river steamers calling out the mark on the leadline. Now he was himself plumbing an unfathomable sea.

Later in the day Phatik's mother burst into the room like a whirlwind, and rocking herself to and fro from side to side began to moan and cry.

Bishambar tried to calm her, but she flung herself on the bed, and cried: 'Phatik, my darling, my darling.'

Phatik stopped his restless movements for a moment. His hands ceased beating up and down. He said: 'Eh?'

The mother cried again: 'Phatik, my darling, my darling.'

Very slowly Phatik's eyes wandered, but he could no longer see the people round his bed. At last he murmured: 'Mother, the holidays have come.'

5

Once There was a King

'Once upon a time there was a king.'

When we were children there was no need to know who the king in the fairy story was. It didn't matter whether he was called Siladitya or Salivahan, whether he lived at Kashi or Kanauj. The thing that made a seven-year-old boy's heart go thump with delight was this one sovereign truth, this reality of all realities: 'Once there was a king.'

But the readers of this modern age are far more exact and exacting. When they hear such an opening to a story, they are at once critical and suspicious. They apply the searchlight of science to its legendary haze and ask: 'Which king?'

The story-tellers also have become more precise. They are no longer content with the old indefinite, 'There was a king,' but assume instead a look of profound learning and begin: 'Once there was a king named Ajatasatru.'

The modern reader's curiosity, however, is not so easily satisfied. He blinks at the author through his scientific spectacles and asks again: 'Which Ajatasatru?'

When we were young, we understood all sweet things; and we could detect the sweets of a fairy story by an unerring science of our own. We never cared for such useless things as knowledge. We only cared for truth. And our unsophisticated little hearts knew well where the Crystal Palace of Truth lay and how to reach it. But today we are expected to write pages of facts, while the truth is simply this:

'There was a king.'

I remember vividly that evening in Calcutta when the fairy story began. It had been raining all day long. The whole city was flooded. In our lane the water was knee-deep. I had a straining hope, which was almost a certainty, that my tutor would be prevented from coming that evening. I sat on the stool in the far corner of the verandah looking down the lane, and my heart beat faster and faster. Every minute I kept my eye on the rain, and when it began to abate, I prayed with all my might: 'Please, God, let it keep on raining till after half-past seven.' For I was quite ready to believe that the only need for rain was to protect one helpless boy one evening in a certain corner of Calcutta from the deadly clutches of his tutor.

If not in answer to my prayer, at least according to some grosser law of nature, the rain did not give over. But, alas, neither did my teacher!

Exactly to the minute, in the turn of the lane, I saw his umbrella approaching. The great bubble of hope burst in my breast, and my heart collapsed. Truly, if there is, after death, a punishment to fit the crime, then my tutor will be born again in my place, and I shall be born in my tutor's.

As soon as I saw his umbrella, I ran as hard as I could to my mother's room. My mother and my grandmother were sitting opposite each other, playing cards by the light of a lamp. I ran into the room, flung myself on the bed beside my mother and said:

'Mother, my tutor has come, and I have such a bad headache; could I do without my lesson today?'

I hope no child will be allowed to read this story and I sincerely trust it will not be used in textbooks, or primers, for junior classes. For what I did was dreadfully bad, and I received no punishment whatever. On the contrary my wicked request was granted.

Mother said to me: 'All right,' and turning to the servant added: 'Tell the tutor that he can go back home.'

It was quite plain that she did not think my illness very serious, for she went on with her game and took no further notice. And I, burying my head in the pillow, laughed to my heart's content. We understood one another, perfectly, my mother and I.

But everyone must know how hard it is for a boy seven years old to keep up the illusion of illness for long. After about a minute I caught hold of grandmother and said: 'Granny, do tell me a story.'

I had to ask many times. Granny and Mother went on playing cards and took no notice. At last Mother said to me: 'Child, don't bother. Wait till we've finished our game.' But I persisted: 'Granny, do tell me a story.' I told Mother she could finish her game tomorrow, that she must let Granny tell me a story there and then.

At last, Mother threw down the cards and said: 'You had better do what he wants. I can't manage him.' Perhaps she remembered that she would have no tiresome tutor the following day, while I should have to be back at those stupid lessons.

As soon as Mother had given way, I rushed at Granny. I seized her hand, and dancing with delight, dragged her inside my mosquito curtain on to the bed. I clutched the bolster with both hands in my excitement, and jumped up and down with joy, and when at last I had become a little quieter, said: 'Now, Granny let's have the story!'

Granny went on, 'And the king had a queen.'

That was good to begin with. He had only one!

It is usual for kings in fairy stories to be extravagant in the number of queens they have. And whenever we hear that there are two queens, our hearts begin to sink. One of them is sure to be unhappy. But in Granny's story there was no danger of that. He had only one queen.

The next detail of Granny's story was that the king had no son. At the age of seven I did not think one need bother if a man had no son. He might only have been in the way.

Nor was I greatly excited when I heard that the king had gone into the forest to practise austerities in order to obtain a son. There was only one thing that would have made me go into the forest, and that was to get away from my tutor!

But the king had left behind with his queen a little girl, who grew up into a beautiful princess.

Twelve years passed away, and the king went on practising austerities, and never thought of his beautiful daughter. The princess had reached the full bloom of her youth. The age of marriage had passed, but the king had not returned. And the queen pined away with grief and cried: 'Is my golden daughter destined to die unmarried? Ah me, what a fate is mine!'

Then the queen sent men to the king, entreating him to come back if only for a single night, and to eat one meal in the palace. And the king consented.

With the greatest care, the queen cooked with her own hand sixty-four dishes. She made a seat for him of sandalwood and arranged the food in plates of gold and cups of silver. The princess stood behind his seat with the peacock-tail fan in her hand. After his twelve years' absence, the king entered the house, and the princess, waving the fan, lighted up all the room with her beauty. The king looked in his daughter's face and forgot even to eat.

At last he asked his queen: 'Pray, who is this girl whose beauty shines as the golden image of the goddess? Whose daughter is she?'

The queen beat her forehead and cried: 'Ah, how evil is my fate! Do you not recognise your own daughter?'

For some time the king remained in silent amazement, but at last he exclaimed: 'My tiny daughter has grown to be a woman.'

'How could it be otherwise?' the queen asked with a sigh. 'Do you not know that twelve years have passed?'

'But why did you not give her in marriage?' asked the king.

'You were away,' the queen replied. 'And how could I find her a suitable husband?'

At this the king, strangely excited, vowed that the first man he saw the following day when he went out of the palace, should marry her.

But the princess merely went on waving her fan of peacock feathers and the king finished his meal.

The next morning, as the king went out of his palace, he saw the son of a Brahman gathering sticks in the forest outside the palace gates. He was about seven or eight years old.

The king said: 'I will marry my daughter to him.'

Who can interfere with a king's command? At once the boy was called, and the marriage garlands were exchanged between him and the princess.

At this point I came up close to my wise Granny and asked her eagerly: 'What then?'

In the bottom of my heart there was a devout wish that I might be that fortunate seven-year-old wood-gatherer. The night resounded with the patter of rain. The earthen lamp by my bedside was burning low. My grandmother's voice droned on as she told the story. And all these things served to create in a corner of my credulous heart the belief that I had been gathering sticks in the dawn of some indefinite time in the kingdom of some unknown king, and that in a moment garlands had been exchanged between me and the princess, beautiful as the Goddess of Grace. She had a gold band on her hair and gold earrings in her ears. She wore a necklace and bracelets of gold, and a golden waist-chain round her waist, and a pair of golden anklets tinkled with the movements of her feet.

If my grandmother had been an author, how many explanations would she not have had to offer of this little story! First of all, everyone would ask why the king remained twelve years in the forest? And then, why should the king's daughter remain unmarried all that time? Such a delay would be regarded as absurd.

Even if my Granny could have got so far without quarrelling with her critics, still there would have been a great hue and cry about the marriage itself. In the first place, it never happened. And in the second, how could there be a marriage between a princess of the warrior caste and a boy of the priestly Brahman caste? Her readers would have imagined at once that the writer was preaching against our social customs in an indirect and unfair way. And they would write letters to the papers.

So I pray with all my heart that my grandmother may be born a grandmother again, and not through some cursed fate be born again in the person of her luckless grandson.

With a throb of joy and delight, I asked Granny: 'What then?'

Granny went on: Then the princess took her little husband away, and built for him a large palace with seven wings, and cherished him there.

I jumped up and down in my bed, clutched the bolster tighter than ever and said: 'What then?'

Granny continued: The little boy went to school and learnt many lessons from his teachers, and as he grew up, the boys in his class began to ask him: 'Who is that beautiful lady living with you in the palace with the seven wings?'

The Brahman's son was eager to know who she was. He could only remember how one day he had been gathering sticks and how a great disturbance had arisen. But all this was so long ago that he had no clear recollection of it.

In this way, four or five years passed. His companions were always asking him: 'Who is that beautiful lady in the palace with the seven wings?' And the Brahman's son would come back from school and sadly say to the princess: 'My school companions always ask me who that beautiful lady is in the palace with the seven wings, and I cannot answer them. Tell me, oh, tell me, who you are!'

The princess said: 'Let it pass untold today. I will tell you some other day.' And every day the Brahman's son would ask: 'Who are you?' and the princess would reply: 'Let it pass untold today. I will tell you some other day.' And so four or five years more went by.

At last the Brahman's son became very impatient and said: 'If you do not tell me today who you are, O beautiful lady, I will leave this palace with the seven wings.' Then the princess said: 'I will certainly tell you tomorrow.'

Next day the Brahman's son, as soon as he came home from school, said: 'Now, tell me who you are.' The princess said: 'Tonight after supper I will tell you when you are in bed.'

The Brahman's son agreed. And he began to count the hours in expectation of the night. And the princess spread white flowers over the golden bed, filled a golden lamp with fragrant oil and lighted it, adorned her hair, and dressing herself in a beautiful robe of blue, began also to count the hours in expectation of the night.

That evening her husband, the Brahman's son, was almost too excited to eat, but when he had finished his supper, he went to the golden bed in the bed-chamber strewn with flowers, and said to himself: 'Tonight I shall surely know who this beautiful lady is in the palace with the seven wings.'

The princess ate what was left over from her husband's supper, and slowly entered the bed-chamber. She had to reveal that very night the identity of the beautiful lady that lived in the palace with the seven wings. And as she went up to the bed to tell him, she found a serpent had crept out of the flowers and had bitten the Brahman's son. Her boy-husband was lying on the bed of flowers, his face pale in death.

My heart suddenly ceased to throb, and I asked with a voice choking with tears: 'What then?'

Granny said: 'Then......'

But what is the use of going on any further with the story? It would only lead to what was more and more impossible. The boy of seven did not know that even though there were some 'What then?' after death, not even the grandmother of a grandmother could tell us all about it.

But the child's faith never admits defeat, and it would snatch at the mantle of Death himself in an attempt to prevent his approach. It would be outrageous for him to think that such a story told on an evening when his teacher was away could come so suddenly to a stop. Therefore the grandmother has to call back her fairy tale from the ever-shut chamber of the great End. And she does it so simply—merely by floating the dead body down the river on a banana stem, and having some incantations read by a magician. But on that rainy night and in the dim light of a lamp, death in the mind of the boy loses all its horror, and seems nothing more than the deep slumber of a single night. When the story ends, the tired eyelids are weighed down with sleep. Thus it is that we send the little body of the child floating on the back of sleep over the still water of time, and then in the morning read a few verses of incantation to restore him to the world of life and light.

6

Master Mashai

: 1 :

*A*dhar Babu lived upon the interest of the capital left him by his father. Only brokers, negotiating loans, came to his drawing room and smoked the silver-chased hookah, or clerks from the attorney's office came to discuss the terms of some mortgage or the amount of certain stamp fees. He was so careful with his money that even the most dogged efforts of the boys from the local football club failed to make any inroads upon his pocket.

At the time this story opens, a new guest came into his household. After a long period of despair, his wife, Nanibala, bore him a son.

The child resembled his mother—he had large eyes, a well-formed nose, and a fair complexion. Ratikanta, Adharlal's protégé summed up the general opinion—'He is worthy of his noble house.' They named him Venugopal.

Never before had Adharlal's wife expressed any opinion on household expenses differing from her husband's. There had been a hot discussion now and then about the propriety of some necessary item, but before this new arrival, she had merely acknowledged defeat with silent contempt. But now Adharlal could no longer maintain his supremacy. He had to give way, little by little, when it was a question of things to be bought for his son.

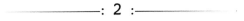

—————: 2 :—————

As Venugopal grew up, his father gradually became accustomed to spend money on him. He engaged an old teacher, with a considerable reputation for learning and also for his success in dragging boys through their examinations, who otherwise would inevitably have failed. But such a training does not lead to the cultivation of amiability. This man tried his best to win the boy's heart, but the little that was left in him of the milk of human kindness had turned sour from the very beginning, and the child repulsed his advances. The mother, in consequence, objected to him strongly, and complained that the very sight of him made her boy ill. In consequence the teacher left.

Just then Haralal made his appearance in dirty clothes and a torn pair of old canvas shoes. Haralal's mother, who was a widow, had kept him with great difficulty at a district school out of the scanty earnings which she made by cooking in strange houses and by husking rice. He had managed to pass the Matriculation examination and had determined to go to college. As a result of semi-starvation, his pinched face tapered unnaturally to a point—like Cape Comorin on the map of India—and the only broad portion of it was his forehead which resembled the range of the Himalayas.

The servant asked Haralal what he wanted, and he answered timidly that he wished to see the master.

The servant answered sharply: 'You can't see him.' When Haralal, at a loss what to do next, was hesitating, Venugopal, who had finished his game in the garden, came suddenly to the door. The servant shouted at Haralal to go away. Quite unaccountably Venugopal grew excited and cried: 'No, he shan't go away.' And he dragged the stranger to his father.

Adharlal had just risen from his midday sleep and was sitting quietly on the upper verandah in his cane-chair, swinging his legs. Ratikanta seated in a chair next to him was enjoying his hookah. He asked Haralal how far he had got in his reading. The young man bent his head and answered that he had passed the Matriculation examination. Ratikanta with a stern look expressed surprise that a boy of his age should be so backward. Harlal kept silent. It was Ratikanta's special pleasure to torture his patron's dependants, whether actual or potential.

Suddenly it struck Adharlal that he would be able to employ this youth for next to nothing as a tutor for his son. He agreed, there and then, to take him on a salary of five rupees a month with board and lodging free.

————: 3 :————

This time the post of tutor was occupied longer than ever before. From the very beginning of their acquaintance Haralal and his pupil became great friends. Never before had Haralal been given such an opportunity of loving a young human creature. His mother had been so poor and dependent, that he had never had the privilege of playing with the children at the houses where she was employed. Hitherto he had not suspected the hidden stores of love which lay accumulating in his heart.

Venu also was glad to find a companion in Haralal. He was the only boy in the house. His two younger sisters were looked down upon, as unworthy of being his playmates. So his new tutor became his only companion, patiently bearing the undivided weight of the tyranny of his child friend.

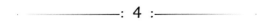

—: **4** :—

Venu was now eleven. Haralal had passed the Intermediate examination, and won a scholarship. He was working hard for his B.A. degree. After college lectures were over, he would take Venu out into the public park and tell him stories about the heroes from Greek history and from Victor Hugo's romances. The child, in spite of his mother's attempt to keep him by her side, used to get quite impatient to run to Haralal after school hours.

This displeased Nanibala. She thought that it was a deep-laid plot of Haralal's to captivate her boy, so that he might remain indefinitely in his post as tutor. One day she talked to him behind the purdah: 'It is your duty to teach my son for an hour or two only in the morning and evening. But why are you always with him? The child has nearly forgotten his own parents. You must understand that a man of your position is no companion for a boy of this house.'

Haralal's voice choked a little as he answered that in future he would be Venu's teacher merely, and would keep away from him at other times.

It was Haralal's usual practice to begin his college study long before dawn. The child would come to him as soon as he had washed. There was a small pool in the garden where they used to feed the fish with puffed rice. Venu was also engaged in building a miniature garden-house, at the corner of the garden, with Lilliputian gates and hedges and gravel paths. When the sun became too hot, they used to go back into the house, where Venu would have his morning lesson from Haralal.

On the day in question Venu had risen earlier than usual, because he wished to hear the end of the story which Haralal had begun the evening before. But he could not find his teacher. When asked about him, the servant at the door said that he had gone out. At lesson time

Venu sat unnaturally quiet. He never even asked Haralal why he had gone out, but went on mechanically with his lessons. When the child was with his mother at breakfast, she asked him what had happened to make him so gloomy, and why he could not eat. Venu did not answer. After his meal his mother caressed him and questioned him repeatedly, Venu burst out crying and said, 'Master Mashai.' His mother asked him, 'What about Master Mashai?' But Venu found it difficult to say in what way his teacher had offended.

So his mother asked him: 'Has your Master Mashai been saying anything to you against *me*?'

But Venu could not understand her question and went away.

—————: **5** :——

Soon after this, there was a theft in Adhar Babu's house. The police were called in to investigate. Even Haralal's trunks were searched. Ratikanta said with meaning: 'The man who steals anything does not hide his ill-gotten gains in his own box.'

Adharlal called his son's tutor and said to him: 'It will not be convenient for me to keep you in this house. From today you will have to live elsewhere, and only come in to teach my son at the usual time.'

At this, Ratikanta drawing at his hookah remarked sagely: 'This is a good proposal—good for both parties.'

Haralal said not a word, but he sent a letter saying that he could no longer remain as tutor to Venu.

When Venu came back from school, he found his tutor's room empty. Even that broken steel trunk of his had vanished. The rope was stretched across the corner, but there were no clothes or towels hanging on it. But on the table, which formerly was strewn with books and papers, stood a bowl containing some gold-fish. On the bowl was a label inscribed with the word 'Venu' in Haralal's handwriting. At once the boy ran up to his father and asked him what had happened. His father told that Haralal had resigned his post. Venu went to his room, flung himself down and began to cry so bitterly that Adharlal could in no way comfort him.

Next day, Haralal was sitting on his wooden bedstead in the hostel, debating whether he should attend his college lectures, when suddenly he saw Adhar Babu's servant coming into his room followed by Venu. Venu at once ran up to him, threw his arms round his neck and asked him to come back to the house.

Haralal could not explain why it was absolutely impossible for him to go back, but, whenever he thought later of those clinging arms and that pleading voice, a lump seemed to rise in his throat.

———: 6 :———

Haralal, after his sad parting from his little friend, found that his mind was unsettled, and that he had but little chance of winning a scholarship, even if he could pass the examination. At the same time, he knew that without the scholarship, he could not continue his studies. So he tried to obtain employment in some office.

Fortunately for him, the English manager of a big mercantile firm took a fancy to him at first sight. After a brief exchange of words, the manager asked him whether he had had any experience, and whether he could bring any testimonials. Haralal could only answer 'No'; nevertheless a post was offered him on a salary of twenty rupees a month, and a sum of fifteen rupees was allowed him in advance to enable him to come properly dressed to the office.

The manager made Haralal work extremely hard. He had to stay on after office hours and sometimes go to his master's house late in the evening. But, in this way, he learnt his work quicker than others and his fellow clerks became jealous of him and tried to injure him, but without effect. As soon as his salary was raised to forty rupees a month, he took a small house in a narrow lane and brought his mother to live with him. Thus happiness came back to his mother after weary years of waiting.

——————: 7 :——————

Haralal's mother frequently said that she would like to see Venugopal, of whom she had heard so much. She wished to prepare some dishes with her own hand and to ask him to come just once to dine with her son. Haralal avoided the subject by saying that his house was not big enough to invite him to.

The news reached Haralal that Venu's mother was dead. He could not wait a moment, but went at once to Adharlal's house to see Venu and from that time onwards they began to see each other frequently.

But times had changed. Venu, stroking his budding moustache, had grown quite the young man of fashion. His friends were numerous, and they suited well his present position. The old dilapidated study chair and ink-stained desk had vanished, and the room now seemed to be bursting with pride at its new acquisitions–its looking-glasses, oleographs, and other furniture. Venu had entered college, but showed no haste to cross the boundary of the Intermediate examination.

Haralal remembered his mother's request to invite Venu to dinner. After great hesitation, he did so. Venugopal, with his handsome face, at once won the mother's heart. But as soon as the meal was over, he became impatient to go, and looking at his gold watch he explained that he had pressing engagements elsewhere. Then he jumped into his carriage, which was waiting at the door, and drove away. Haralal with a sigh said to himself that he would never invite him again.

——————: 8 :——————

One day, on returning from office, Haralal noticed a man sitting in the dark room on the ground floor of his house. He would perhaps have passed him by, had not the heavy scent of some foreign perfume attracted his attention. Haralal asked who was there, and the answer came:

'It is I, Master Mashai.'

'What is the matter, Venu?' said Haralal. 'When did you come here?'

'I came hours ago,' said Venu. 'I did not know that you returned so late.'

They went upstairs together and Haralal lighted the lamp and asked Venu how he was getting on. Venu replied that his college classes were becoming a fearful bore, and his father did not realise how dreadfully hard it was for him to go in the same class year after year, with students much younger than himself. Haralal asked him what he wished to do. Venu then told him that he wanted to go to England and become a barrister. He gave an instance of a student, much less advanced in his college course, who was getting ready to go. Haralal asked him if he had received his father's permission. Venu replied that his father would not hear a word of it until he had passed the Intermediate examination, and that was an impossibility in his present frame of mind. Haralal suggested that he himself might go and try to talk over Venu's father.

'No,' said Venu, 'I can never allow that!'

Haralal asked Venu to stay to dinner, and while they were waiting he gently placed his hand on Venu's shoulder and said: 'Venu, you should not quarrel with your father, or leave home.'

Venu jumped up angrily and said that if he was not welcome, he would go elsewhere. Haralal caught him by the hand and implored him not go away without dining. But Venu snatched his hand away and was on the point of leaving the room when Haralal's mother brought the food in on a tray. Seeing Venu about to leave, she pressed him to remain, and he did so, but with bad grace.

While he was seated at dinner, the sound of a carriage was heard stopping at the door. First a servant entered the room with creaking shoes and then Adhar Babu himself. At the sight of his father, Venu's face became pale. The mother left the room as soon as she saw strangers enter. Adhar Babu began to abuse Haralal in a voice thick with anger: 'Ratikanta gave me full warning, but I could not believe that you were a man of such devilish cunning. So, you think you're going to live upon Venu? This is sheer kidnapping, and I shall prosecute you in the Police Court.'

Venu silently followed his father out of the house.

————: 9 :————

The firm in which Haralal was employed, began to buy up large quantities of rice and *dal* from the country districts. To purchase this produce, Haralal had to take the cash every Saturday morning by the early train and pay it out. There were special centres where the brokers and middlemen used to come with their receipt and account for settlement. Some discussion had taken place in the office about Haralal being entrusted with this work without any security, but the manager undertook all the responsibility and said that security was not needed. This special work used to go on from the middle of December to the middle of April, and Haralal frequently returned from it very late at night.

One day, after his return from work, his mother told him that Venu had called and that she had persuaded him to dine with them. This had happened more than once. The mother said that it was because Venu missed his own mother, and tears came into her eyes as she spoke about it.

On one such occasion Venu waited for Haralal to return and had a long talk with him.

'Master Mashai!' he said, 'Father has lately become so irritable that I can no longer live with him. And, besides, I know that he is thinking of marrying again. Ratikanta is seeking a suitable match, and they are always conspiring about it. There used to be a time when my father would be anxious if I were absent from home even for a few hours. Now, if I am away for more than a week, he takes no notice, indeed, he is greatly relieved. If his marriage takes place, I feel that I cannot live in the house any longer. You must show me a way out of this. I want to become independent.'

Haralal felt deeply grieved, but he could not see how he could help his former pupil. Venu said that he was determined to go to England and become a barrister. Somehow or other he must get the passage money out of his father: he might borrow it on a note of hand and then his father would have to pay when the creditors filed a suit.

With this borrowed money he might get away, and when he was in England his father was bound to send money to meet his expenses.

'But,' Haralal asked, 'who is there that would advance you the money?'

'You!' said Venu.

'I,' exclaimed Haralal in amazement.

'Yes,' said Venu, 'I've seen the servant bringing heaps of money here in bags.'

'The servant and the money belong to someone else.'

Haralal explained why the money came to his house at night, like birds to their nest, to be scattered next morning.

'But can't the manager advance the sum?' Venu asked.

'He may do so,' said Haralal, 'if your father stands security.'

At this point the discussion ended.

: 10 :

One Friday night a carriage and pair stopped before Haralal's lodging house. When Venu was announced, Haralal was sitting on the floor of his bedroom, counting some money. Venu entered dressed in an unaccustomed manner. He had discarded his Bengali dress and was wearing a Parsee coat and trousers and on his head was a cap. Rings glittered on most of the fingers of both hands, and a thick gold chain was hanging round his neck; there was a gold watch in his pocket, and diamond studs could be seen peeping from his shirt sleeves. Haralal at once asked him what was the matter and why he was wearing such clothes.

Venu replied: 'My father is to be married tomorrow. He tried hard to keep it from me, but I found it out. I asked him to allow me to go to our garden-house at Barrackpore for a few days, and he was only too glad to get rid of me so easily. I am going there, and I wish to God I never had to come back.'

Venu, seeing that Haralal looked pointedly at the rings on his fingers, explained that they had belonged to his mother. Haralal then asked him if he had already had dinner. He answered, 'Yes, haven't you?'

'No,' said Haralal, 'I cannot leave this room until I have safely locked up all the money in this iron chest.'

'Go and have dinner,' said Venu, 'while I keep guard here; your mother will be waiting for you.'

For a moment Haralal hesitated, and then he went out and dined. In a short time he came back with his mother and the three of them sat talking among the bags of money. When it was nearly midnight, Venu looked at his watch and jumped up, saying that he would miss his train. He then asked Haralal to keep his rings and his watch and chain until he asked for them again. Haralal put them all together in a leather bag which he placed in the iron safe, whereupon Venu left the house.

The canvas bags containing the currency notes had already been placed in the safe: only the loose coins remained to be counted over and put away with the rest.

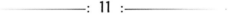

—: 11 :—

Haralal lay down near the door of the room, placed the key under his pillow, and went to sleep. He dreamt that from behind the curtain Venu's mother was loudly reproaching him. Her words were indistinct, but rays of different colours from the jewels which she wore kept piercing the curtain like violently vibrating needles. Haralal struggled to call Venu, but his cry seemed to stick in his throat. At last, the curtain fell noisily down. Haralal started up from his sleep and found that all was dark around him. A sudden gust of wind had flung the window open and blow out the light. Haralal was covered with perspiration. He re-lighted the lamp and saw, by the clock, that it was four in the morning. There was no time to go to sleep again; for he had to get ready to start.

He had just washed his face and hands, when his mother called from her own room, 'Baba, why are you up so early?'

It was a habit of Haralal to see his mother's face the first thing in the morning in order to bring a blessing on the day. His mother said to him: 'I was dreaming that you were going out to bring home a bride.' Haralal then went back to his bedroom and began to take out the bags containing the silver and the currency notes.

Suddenly his heart seemed to stop beating. Three of the bags appeared to be empty. He knocked them against the iron safe, but this only proved his fear to be true. Nevertheless he opened them and shook them with all his might. But he could find nothing in them but two letters from Venu, one of which was addressed to his father and the other to himself.

Haralal tore open his own letter and tried to read it. But the words seemed to run into one another. He trimmed the lamp, but felt that he could not understand what he read. Yet the purport of the letter was clear. Venu had taken three thousand rupees in currency notes, and had started for England. The steamer was to sail before daybreak that very morning. The letter ended with the words: 'I am explaining everything in a letter to my father. He will pay off the debt; and then, again, my mother's ornaments, which I have left in your care, will more than cover the amount I have taken.'

Haralal locked up his room and hiring a carriage hurried to the jetty. But he did not know even the name of the steamer which Venu had taken. He ran the whole length of the wharves from Prinsep's Ghat to Metiaburuj. He found two steamers had sailed for England early that morning. It was impossible for him to find out which of them carried Venu, or how to reach him.

When Haralal returned home the sun was strong and the whole of Calcutta was awake. Everything before his eyes seemed blurred. He felt as if he were pushing against a fearful obstacle, unembodies but piti-less. His mother came on to the verandah and asked him anxiously where he had been. With a strained laugh he said to her, 'To bring home a bride for myself!' And then he fainted away.

After some time, Haralal recovered consciousness, and opening his eyes asked his mother to leave him. Entering his room he shut the door, while his mother sat at the door of the verandah in the fierce glare of the sun. She kept calling to him fitfully, almost mechanically, 'Baba, Baba!'

As usual, the servant came from the manager's office and knocked at the door, saying that they would miss the train if they did not start at once. Haralal called from inside: 'Cannot start this morning.'

'Then, when are we to go, sir?'

'I will tell you later on.'

The servant went downstairs with a gesture of impatience.

Suddenly Heralal thought of the ornaments which Venu had left behind. He had completely forgotten about them, but with the thought came instant relief. He took he leather bag containing them, and also Venu's letter to his father, and left the house.

Before he reached Adharlal's house he could hear the band, playing for the wedding, yet on entering could feel that there had been some disturbance. Haralal was told that there had been a theft the night before and that some of the servants were suspected. Adhar Babu was sitting in the upper verandah, flushed with anger and Ratikanta was sitting near him smoking his hookah. Haralal said to Adhar Babu, 'I have something to tell you in private.' Adharlal's anger flared up, and he shouted: 'I have no time now!' He was afraid that Haralal had come to borrow money or to ask his help. Ratikanta suggested that if Haralal felt uncomfortable in making any request in his presence he would leave. Adharlal told him angrily to sit where he was. Then Haralal handed over the bag which Venu had left behind. Adharlal asked what was inside, so Haralal opened it and gave him the contents.

Then Adhar Babu said with a sneer: 'It's a praying business that you two have started—you and your former pupil! You were certain that the stolen property would be traced, and so you bring it to me to claim a reward!'

Haralal presented the letter which Venu had written to his father, but this only made Adharlal the more furious.

'What's all this?' he shouted, 'I'll call the police! My son has not yet come of age, and *you* have smuggled him out of the country! I'll bet my soul you've lent him a few hundred rupees, and then taken a note of hand for three thousand! But I am not going to be bound by *this!*'

'I have not advanced him a single pice,' protested Haralal.

'Then how did he find it?' asked Adharlal. 'Do you mean to tell me he broke open your safe and stole it.'

Haralal stood silent, while Ratikanta sarcastically remarked: 'I don't believe this fellow ever set hands on so much as three thousand rupees in his life.'

When Haralal left the house, it seemed to him that he had passed beyond all possibility of fear or anxiety. His mind seemed to refuse to work. As soon as he entered the lane he saw a carriage waiting before his house. For a moment he felt certain that it was Venu's. It was impossible to believe that his calamity could be so hopelessly final.

Haralal went quickly up to the carriage, but found an English assistant from the firm sitting inside it. The man got down when he saw Haralal, seized him by the wrist and asked him: 'Why didn't you leave by the train this morning? The servant had told the manager his suspicions and he had sent this man to find out.

Haralal answered: 'Because I found that notes to the value of three thousand rupees were missing.'

The man asked how that could have happened, but Haralal was silent.

Seeing his embarrassment, the assistant said to Haralal: 'Let us go upstairs together and see where you keep your money.' So they went up to the room, counted the money and made a thorough search of the house.

When Haralal's mother saw this she could contain herself no longer. She therefore came up to the stranger and asked her son what had happened. The man answered in broken Hindustani that some money had been stolen.

'Stolen!' the mother cried, 'Why! How could it be stolen? Who would do such a dastardly thing?' But Haralal forbade her to speak.

The man collected the remainder of the money and told Haralal to come with him to the manager. The mother barred the way and said:

'Sir, where are you taking my son? I have done everything in my power, I have even starved myself so that he might be brought up to do honest work. My son would never touch money that was not his own.'

The Englishman, not knowing Bengali, could only reply, '*Achcha! Achcha!*' Haralal entreated his mother not to be anxious; he would explain it all to the manager and soon be back again. His mother, distressed by the fact that her son had eaten nothing all morning, begged him to remain a moment to break his fast, but Haralal disregarding her appeal, stepped into the carriage and drove away, and the mother in the anguish of her heart sank to the ground.

When Haralal came into the manager's presence, he was asked: 'Tell me the truth, what did happen?' But Haralal could only reply, 'I haven't taken any money.'

'I fully believe it,' said the manager, 'but surely you know who has taken it.'

Haralal remained silent, with his eyes on the ground.

'Somebody,' said the manager, 'must have taken it with your connivance.'

'Nobody,' replied Haralal, 'could take it away with my knowledge unless he first took my life.'

'Look here, Haralal,' said the manager, 'I trusted you completely. I took no security. I employed you in a post of great responsibility. Every one in the office was against me for doing so. The three thousand rupees is a small concern, but the shame of all this to me is a great matter. I will do one thing. I will give you the whole day to bring back this money. If you do so, I shall say nothing about it and I shall keep you on in your post.'

It was eleven o'clock, when Haralal with bent head walked out of the office, and left his fellow-clerks to exult meanly over his disgrace.

'What can I *do*? What can I *do*'? Haralal repeated to himself, the sun's heat pouring down as he walked along like one dazed. At last his mind ceased to think at all about what could be done, but he continued to walk mechanically.

This city of Calcutta, which offered its shelter to thousands upon thousands of men, had become like a steel-trap. He could see no way out. The whole body of people was conspiring to surround and hold him captive—this most insignificant of men, whom no one knew. Nobody had any special grudge against him, yet everybody was his enemy. The crowd passed by, brushing against him: clerks from different offices ate their lunch on the roadside out of plates made of leaves: a tired wayfarer on the Maidan was lying under the shade of a tree, with one hand beneath his head and one leg crossed over the other: up-country women, crowded into hackney carriages, were on their way to the temple: a chuprassi came up with a letter and asked him the address on the envelope—so the afternoon went by, till one by one the offices began to close. Carriages started off in all directions, carrying people back to their homes. The clerks, packed tightly on the seats of the trams, looked at the theatre advertisements as they returned home. It came into his mind that he was no longer a unit in this throng.—no work would engage him all day long, and there would come no pleasant evening release from toil. He had no need to hurry to catch the homeward tram. All the busy occupations of the city—the buildings—the horses and carriages—the incessant traffic—seemed sometimes to swell into dreadful reality, and at other times, to subside into the shadowy unreal.

Haralal had eaten no food, taken no rest, nor sheltered from the sun all that day.

The lamps in one street after another were lighted till it seemed to him that a pervading darkness, like some demon, was keeping its eyes wide open to watch every movement of its victim. Haralal had not the energy even to enquire how late it was. The veins on his forehead throbbed, and he felt as if his head must burst. Through paroxysms of pain, which alternated with the apathy of dejection, one thought came again and again from among the innumerable multitudes in that vast city, the image of only one person rose before his mental vision, and one name alone found its way through his dry throat—'Mother?'

He said to himself, 'In the depth of night when no one is awake to arrest me—me, the least of all men—I will silently creep to my mother's arms and fall asleep, and may I never wake again!'

Haralal's one trouble was lest some police officer should molest him in the presence of his mother and thus prevent him from going home. When at last it became an agony for him to walk further, he hailed a carriage. The driver asked him where he wanted to go. He said: 'Nowhere. I want to drive across the Maidan to breathe some fresh air.' The man at first did not believe him and was about to drive on, when Haralal put a rupee into his hand as earnest of payment. Thereupon the driver crossed, and then recrossed the Maidan from one side to the other, by different roads.

Heralal laid his throbbing head on the side of the open window of the carriage and closed his eyes. Slowly all the pain abated. A deep and intense peace filled his heart and supreme deliverance seemed to embrace him on every side. It was *not* true—this day's despair which threatened to drag him into utter helplessness. It was *not* true, it was false. He knew now that it was only a vain fear that his mind had conjured up from nothing. Deliverance was in the infinite sky and there was no end to peace. No King or Emperor in the world had the power to keep captive his nonentity, this Haralal. In the sky, surrounding his emancipated heart on every side, he felt the presence of his mother, that one poor woman. She seemed to grow and grow till she filled the infinity of darkness. All the roads and buildings and shops of Calcutta gradually became enveloped by her. In her presence all his pain vanished; thought, consciousness itself, closed. It seemed as though a bubble filled with the hot vapour of pain had burst, and now there was neither darkness nor light, but only one tensefulness.

The Cathedral clock struck one. The driver called out impatiently: 'Babu, my horse can't go on any longer. Where do you want to go?'

There came no answer.

The driver came down and shook Haralal and asked him again where he wanted to go.

There came no answer.

And this was a question that never received its answer from Haralal.

7

Subha

$\mathcal{W}$hen the girl was given the name of Subhashini, who could have guessed that she would be dumb when she grew up? Her two elder sisters were Sukheshini and Suhashini, and for the sake of uniformity her father had named his youngest girl Subhashini. She was called Subha for short.

Her two elder sisters had been married with the usual difficulties in finding husbands and providing dowries, and now the youngest daughter lay like a silent weight upon the heart of her parents. People seemed to think that, because she did not speak, therefore she did not feel; they discussed her future and their anxiety concerning it even in her presence. She had understood from her earliest childhood that God had sent her like a curse to her father's house, so she withdrew herself from ordinary people and tried to live apart. If only they would all forget her, she felt she could endure it. But who can forget pain?

Night and day her parents' minds ached with anxiety on her account. Her mother especially looked upon her as a deformity. To a mother, a daughter is a more closely intimate part of herself than a son can be and a fault in her is a source of personal shame. Banikantha, Subha's father, loved her rather better than he did his other daughters; her mother almost hated her as a stain upon her own body.

If Subha lacked speech, she did not lack a pair of large dark eyes, shaded with long lashes; and her lips trembled like a leaf in response to any thought that arose in her mind.

When we express our thoughts in words, the medium is not found easily. There must be a process of translation, which is often inexact, and then we fall into error. But black eyes need no translating; the mind itself throws a shadow upon them. In them, thought opens or shuts, shines forth or goes out in darkness, hangs steadfast like the setting moon or like the swift and restless lightning illumines all quarters of the sky. Those who from birth have had no other speech than the trembling of their lips learn a language of the eyes, endless in expression, deep as the sea, clear as the heavens, wherein play dawn and sunset, light and shadow. The dumb have a lonely grandeur like Nature's own. Wherefore the other children almost dreaded Subha and never played with her. She was silent and companionless as the noontide.

She lived in a small village called Chandipur. The river on whose bank it stood was small for a river of Bengal, and kept to its narrow bounds like a daughter of the middle class. This busy streak of water never overflowed its banks, but went about its duties as though it were a member of every family in the villages besides it. On either side were houses and banks shaded with trees. So stepping from her queenly throne, the river-goddess became a garden deity of each home, and forgetful of herself performed her task of endless benediction with swift and cheerful feet.

Banikantha's house looked out upon the stream. Every hut and stack in the place could be seen by the passing boatmen. I know not if amid these signs of worldly wealth anyone noticed the little girl who, when her work was done, stole away to the waterside and sat there.

But here Nature herself made up for her want of speech and spoke for her. The murmur of the brook, the voice of the village folk, the songs of the boatmen, the cry of the birds and the rustle of trees mingled and were one with the trembling of her heart. They became one vast wave of sound which beat upon her restless soul. This murmur movement of Nature was the dumb girl's language; that speech of the dark eyes, which the long lashes shaded, was the language of the world about her. From the trees, where the cicala chirped, to the quiet stars, there was nothing but signs and gestures, weeping and sighing. And in the deep mid-noon, when the boatmen and fisherfolk had gone to their dinner, when the villagers slept and the birds were still, when the ferry-boats were idle, when the great busy world paused in its toil and became suddenly a lonely, awful giant, then beneath the vast impressive heavens there were only dumb Nature and a dumb girl, sitting very silent—one under the spreading sunlight, the other where a small tree cast its shadow.

But Subha was not altogether without friends. In the stall were two cows, Sarbbashi and Panguli. They had never heard their names from her lips, but they knew her footfall. Though she could form no words, she murmured lovingly and they understood her gentle murmuring better than all speech. When the fondled them or scolded or coaxed them, they understood her better than men could do. Subha would come to the shed and throw her arms round Sarbbashi's neck; she would rub her cheek against her friend's and Panguli would turn her great kind eyes and lick her face. The girl visited them regularly three times a day, and at many an odd moment as well. Whenever she heard any words that hurt her, she would come to these dumb friends even though it might not be the hour for a regular visit. It was as though they guessed her anguish of spirit from her look of quiet sadness. Coming close to her, they would rub their horns softly against her arms, and in dumb, puzzled fashion try to comfort her. Besides these, there were goats and a kitten; but Subha had not the same equal friendship with them, though they showed the same attachment. Every time it got a chance, night or day, the kitten would jump into her lap, and settle down to slumber, and show its appreciation of an aid to sleep as Subha drew her soft fingers over its neck and back.

Subha had a comrade also among the higher animals, and it is hard to say what were the girl's relations with him; for he could speak, and his gift of speech left them without any common language. He was the youngest boy of the Gosains, Pratap by name, an idle fellow. After long effort, his parents had abandoned the hope of his ever making a living. Now losers have this advantage, that though their own folk disapprove of them they are generally popular with everyone else. Having no work to chain them, they became public property. Just as every town needs an open space where all may breathe, so a village needs two or three gentlemen of leisure, who can give time to all; then, if we are lazy and want a companion, one is to hand.

Pratap's chief ambition was to catch fish. He managed to waste a lot of time this way and might be seen almost any afternoon so employed. It was thus most often that he met Subha. Whatever he was about, he liked a companion; and, when one is trying to catch fish, a silent companion is best of all. Pratap respected Subha for her silence, and, as everyone called her Subha, he showed his affection by calling her Su. Subha used to sit beneath a tamarind tree, and Pratap, a little distance off, would cast his line. Pratap took with him a small allowance of betel, and Subha prepared it for him. And I think that, sitting there and gazing a long while, she desired ardently to bring some great help to Pratap, to be a real aid, to prove by any means that she was not a useless burden in the world. But there was nothing to do. Then she turned to the Creator in prayer for some rare power, that by an astonishing miracle she might startle Pratap into exclaiming: 'My! I never dreamt our Su could do this!'

Only think, if Subha had been a water-nymph, she might have risen slowly from the river, bringing the gem of the snake's crown to the landing-place. Then Pratap, leaving his paltry fishing, might have dived into the lower world, and seen there, on a golden bed in a palace, of silver, whom else but dumb little Su, Banikantha's child! Yes, our Su, the only daughter of the king of that shining city of jewels! But that might not be, it was impossible. Not that anything is really impossible, but Su had been born, not into the royal house of Patalpur, but into Banikantha's family, and thus she knew of no means by which she might astonish the Gosains' boy.

She grew up, and little by little began to find herself. A new inexpressible consciousness like a tide from the central places of the sea, when the moon is full, swept through her. She saw herself, questioned herself, but no answer came that she could understand.

Late one night, when the moon was full, she slowly opened her door, and timidly peeped out. Nature, herself at full moon, like lonely Subha, was looking down on the sleeping earth. Subha's strong young life beat within her; joy and sadness filled her being to its brim: she had felt unutterably lonely before but her feeling of loneliness was this moment as its intensest. Her heart was heavy and she could not speak. At the skirts of this silent troubled Mother, there stood a silent troubled girl.

The thought of her marriage filled her parents with anxious care. People blamed them, and even talked of making them outcastes. Banikantha was well off; his family even had fish-curry twice daily, and consequently he did not lack enemies. Then the women interfered, and Bani went away for a few days. Presently he returned and said: 'We must go to Calcutta.'

They got ready to go to this strange place. Subha's heart was heavy with tears, like a mist-wrapt dawn. With a vague fear that had been gathering for days, she dogged her father and mother like a dumb animal. With her large eyes wide open, she scanned their faces as though she wished to learn something. But not a word did they vouchsafe. One afternoon in the midst of all this, as Pratap was fishing, he laughed: 'So then, Su, they have caught your bridegroom, and you are going to be married! Mind you don't forget me altogether!' Then he turned his mind again to his fishing. As a stricken doe looks in the hunter's face, asking in silent agony: 'What have I done to harm you?' so Subha looked at Pratap. That day she sat no longer beneath her tree. Banikantha, having finished his nap, was smoking in his bedroom when Subha dropped at his feet and burst out weeping as she gazed towards him. Banikantha tried to comfort her and his own cheek grew wet with tears.

It was settled that on the morrow they should go to Calcutta. Subha went to the cowshed to bid farewell to the comrades of her childhood. She fed them from her hand; she clasped their necks; she looked into their faces, and tears fell fast from the eyes which spoke for her. That night was the tenth of the new moon. Subha left her room, and flung herself down on her grassy couch besides the river she loved so much. It was as if she threw her arms about the Earth, her strong, silent mother, and tried to say: 'Do not let me leave you, mother. Put your arms about me, as I have put mine about you, and hold me fast.'

One day, in a house in Calcutta, Subha's mother dressed her up with great care. She imprisoned her hair, knotting it up in laces, she hung her about with ornaments, and did her best to kill her natural beauty. Subha's eyes filled with tears. Her mother, fearing they would grow swollen with weeping, scolded her harshly, but the tears disregarded the scolding. The bridegroom came with a friend to inspect the bride. Her parents were dizzy with anxiety and fear when they saw the God arrive to select the beast for his sacrifice. Behind the stage, the mother called her instructions aloud, so that her daughter's weeping redoubled, before she sent her into the examiner's presence. The great man, after looking her up and down a long time, observed: 'Not so bad.'

He took special note of her tears, and thought she must have a tender heart. He put it to her credit in the account, arguing that the heart, which today was distressed at leaving her parents, would presently prove a useful possession. Like the oyster's pearls, the child's tears only increased her value, and he made no other comment.

The almanac was consulted, and the marriage took place on an auspicious day. Having delivered their dumb girl into another's hands, Subha's parents returned home. Thank God! Their caste in this world and their safety in the next were assured! The bridegroom's work lay in the west, and shortly after the marriage he took his wife thither.

In less than ten days everyone knew that the bride was dumb! At least if anyone did not, it was not her fault, for she deceived no one.

Her eyes told them everything, though no one understood her. She looked on every hand, but found no speech; she missed the faces, familiar from birth, of those who had understood a dumb girl's language. In her silent heart there sounded an endless, voiceless weeping, which only the Searcher of Hearts could hear.

8

The Babus of Nayanjore

Once upon a time the Babus of Nayanjore were famous landholders. They were noted for their princely extravagance. They would tear off the rough border of their Dacca muslin, because it rubbed against their delicate skin. They would spend many thousands of rupees over the wedding of a kitten. And on a certain grand occasion it is alleged that in order to turn night into day, they lighted countless lamps and showered silver threads from the sky to imitate sunlight.

Those were the days before the flood. The flood came. The line of succession among these old-world Babus, with their lordly habits, could not continue for long. Like a lamp, with too many wicks burning, the oil flared away quickly, and the light went out.

Kailas Babu, our neighbour, is the last flicker of this extinct magnificence. Before he grew up, his family had very nearly burned itself out. When his father died, there was one dazzling outburst of funeral extravagance, and then insolvency. The property was sold to liquidate the debt. What little ready money was left was altogether insufficient to keep up the ancestral splendours.

Kailas Babu left Nayanjore and came to Calcutta. His son did not remain long in this world of faded glory. He died, leaving behind him an only daughter.

In Calcutta we are Kailas Babu's neighbours. Curiously enough our own family history is just the opposite of his. My father made his money by his own exertions, and prided himself on never spending a penny more than was necessary. His clothes were those of a working man, and his hands also. He never had any inclination to earn the title of Babu by extravagant display; and I, this only son, am grateful to him for that. He gave me the very best education, and I was able to make my way in the world. I am not ashamed of the fact that I am a self-made man. Crisp notes in my safe are dearer to me than a long pedigree in an empty family chest.

I believe this was why I disliked seeing Kailas Babu drawing his heavy cheques on the public credit from the bankrupt bank of his ancient Babu reputation. I used to fancy that he looked down on me, because my father had earned money by manual labour.

I ought to have noticed that no one but myself showed any vexation towards Kailas Babu. Indeed it would have been difficult to find an old man who did less harm than he. He was always ready with his kindly little acts of courtesy in times of sorrow or joy. He would join in all the ceremonies and religious observances of his neighbours. His familiar smile would greet young and old alike. His politeness in asking details about domestic affairs was untiring. The friends who met him in the street were ready perforce to be button-holed, while a long string of remarks of this kind followed one another from his lips:

'I am delighted to see you, my dear friend. Are you quite well? How is Sashi? And Dada—is he all right? Do you know, I've only just heart that Madhu's son has got fever. How is he? Have you heard? And Hari Charan Babu—I have not seen him for a long time—I hope he is not ill. What's the matter with Rakhal? And er—er, how are the ladies of your family?'

Kailas Babu was neat and spotless in his dress on all occasions though his supply of clothes was sorely limited. Every day he used to air his shirts and vests and coats and trousers carefully, and put them out in the sun, along with his bed-quilt, his pillow-case, and the small carpet on which he always sat. After airing them he would shake them, and brush them, and put them carefully away. His little bits of furniture made his small room presentable, and hinted that there was more in reserve if needed. Very often, for want of a servant, he would shut up his house for a while. Then he would iron out his shirts and linen, and do other little menial tasks. He would then open his door and receive his friends again.

Though Kailas Babu, as I have said, had lost all his land, he had still some family heirlooms left. There was a silver cruet for sprinkling scented water, a filigree box for otto-of-roses, a small gold salver, a costly antique shawl, and the old-fashioned ceremonial dress and ancestral turban. These he had rescued with the greatest difficulty from the moneylenders' clutches. On every suitable occasion he would bring them out in state, and thus try to save the world-famed dignity of the Babus of Nayanjore. At heart the most modest of men, in his daily speech he regarded it as a sacred offering, due to his rank, to give free play to his family pride. His friends would encourage this with kindly good-humour, and it gave them great amusement.

The people of the neighbourhood soon learnt to call him their Thakur Dada. They would flock to his house and sit with him for hours together. To prevent his incurring any expense, one or other of his friends would bring him tobacco and say: 'Thakur Dada, this morning some tobacco was sent to me from Gaya. Do try it and see how you like it.'

Thakur Dada would smoke it and say it was excellent. He would then proceed to tell of a certain exquisite tobacco which they once smoked in the old days at Nayanjore that cost a guinea an ounce.

'I wonder,' he used to say, 'if anyone would like to try it now. I have some left, and can get it at once.'

Everyone knew that, if they asked for it, then somehow or other the key of the cupboard would be missing; or else Ganesh, his old family servant, had put it away somewhere.

'You never can be sure,' he would add, 'where things go to when servants are about. Now, this Ganesh of mine—I can't tell you what a fool he is, but I haven't the heart to dismiss him.'

Ganesh, for the credit of the family, was quite ready to bear all the blame without a word.

One of the company usually said at this point: 'Never mind, Thakur Dada. Please don't trouble to look for it. The tobacco we're smoking will do quite well. The other would be too strong.'

Then Thakur Dada would be relieved and settle down again, and the talk would go on.

When his guests got up to go away, Thakur Dada would accompany them to the door and say to them on the doorstep: 'Oh, by the way, when are you all coming to dine with me?'

One or other of us would answer: 'Not just yet Thakur Dada, not just yet. We'll fix a day later.'

'Quite right,' he would answer. 'Quite right. We had much better wait till the rains come. It's too hot now. And a grand dinner, such as I should want to give you, would upset us in weather like this.'

But when the rains did come, everyone was very careful not to remind him of his promise. If the subject was brought up, some friend would suggest gently, that it was very inconvenient to get about when the rains were so severe, and therefore it would be much better to wait till they were over. Thus the game went on.

Thakur Dada's poor house was much too small for his position, and we used to condole with him about it. His friends would assure him they quite understood his difficulties: it was next to impossible to get a decent house in Calcutta. Indeed, they had all been looking out for years for a house to suit him. But, I need hardly add, no friend had been foolish enough to find one. Thakur Dada used to say, with a sigh of resignation: 'Well, well, I suppose I shall have to put up with this house after all.' Then he would add with a genial smile: 'But, you know,

I could never bear to be away from my friends. I must be near you. That really compensates for everything.'

Somehow I felt all this very deeply indeed. I suppose the real reason was that, when a man is young, stupidity appears to him the worst of crimes. Kailas Babu was not really stupid. In ordinary business matters everyone was ready to consult him. But with regard to Nayanjore his utterances certainly seemed void of common sense. Since, out of amused affection for him, no one contradicted his impossible statements, he refused to keep them within bounds. When people recounted in his hearing the glorious history of Nayanjore, with absurd exaggerations, he would accept all they said with the utmost gravity, and never doubted even in his dreams, that anyone could disbelieve it.

When I sit down and try to analyse the thoughts and feelings that I had towards Kailas Babu, I see that there was a still deeper reason for my dislike; which I shall now explain.

Though I am the son of a rich man, and might have wasted time at college, my industry was such that I took my M.A. degree at Calcutta University when quite young. My moral character was flawless. In addition, my outward appearance was so handsome, that if I were to call myself beautiful, it might be thought a mark of self-esteem but could not be considered an untruth.

There could be no question that I was regarded by parents generally as a very eligible match among the young men of Bengal. I myself was quite clear on the point and had determined to obtain my full value in the marriage market. When I pictured my choice, I had before my mind's eye a wealthy father's only daughter, extremely beautiful and highly educated. Proposals came pouring into me from far and near; large sums in cash were offered. I weighed these offers with rigid impartiality in the delicate scales of my own estimation. But there was no one fit to be my partner. I became convinced with the poet Bhaba-vuti, that:

In this world's endless time and boundless space
One may be born at last to match my sovereign grace.

But in this puny modern age, and this contracted space of modern Bengal, it was doubtful whether the peerless creature existed.

Meanwhile my praises were sung in many tunes, and in different metres, by designing parents.

Whether I was pleased with their daughters or not, this worship which they offered was never unpleasing. I used to regard it as my proper due, because I was so good. We are told that when the gods withhold their boons from mortals, they still expect their worshippers to pay them fervent honour and are angry if it is withheld. I had that divine expectancy strongly developed.

I have already mentioned that Thakur Dada had an only grand-daughter. I had seen her many times, but had never thought her beautiful. No idea had ever entered my mind that she would be a possible partner for me. All the same it seemed quite certain to me that some day or other Kailas Babu would offer her, with all due worship, as an oblation at my shrine. Indeed—this was the inner secret of my dislike—I was thoroughly annoyed that he had not done so already.

I heard that Thakur Dada had told his friends that the Babus of Nayanjore never craved a boon. Even if the girl remained unmarried, he would not break the family tradition. It was this arrogance of his that made me angry. My indignation smouldered for some time. But I remained perfectly silent and bore it with the utmost patience, because I was so good.

As lightning accompanies thunder, so in my character a flash of humour was mingled with the mutterings of my wrath. It was, of course, impossible for me to punish the old man merely in order to give vent to my rage; and for a long time I did nothing at all. But suddenly one day such an amusing plan came into my head, that I could not resist the temptation to carry it into effect.

I have already said that many of Kailas Babu's friends used to flatter the old man's vanity without stint. One, who was a retired Government servant, had told him that whenever he saw the Chota Lât Sahib he asked for the latest news about the Babus of Nayanjore and the Chota Lât had been heard to say that in all Bengal the only really respectable families were those of the Maharaja of Cossipore and the Babus of Nayanjore. When the monstrous falsehood was told to Kailas Babu, he was very proud and often repeated the story. And wherever after that he met this Government servant in company, he would ask, among other things:

'Oh! Er—by the way, how is the Chota Lât Sahib? Quite well, did you say? Ah yes, I am so delighted to hear it! And the dear Mem Sahib, is she quite well too? Ah, yes! And the little children—are they quite well also? Ah yes! that's very good news! Be sure and give them my compliments when you see them.'

Kailas Babu frequently expressed his intention of going some day and paying a visit to the Lât Sahib. But it may be taken for granted that many Chota Lâts and Burra Lâts also would come and go, and much water would flow under the Hooghly bridges, before the family coach of Nayanjore would be furbished up to take Kailas Babu to Government House.

One day I took him aside and whispered to him: 'Thakur Dada, I was at the Levee yesterday, and the Chota Lât Sahib happened to mention the Babus of Nayanjore. I told him that Kailas Babu had come to town. Do you know, he was terribly hurt because you hadn't called? He told me he was going to put etiquette on one side and pay you a private visit this very afternoon.'

Anybody else would have seen through this plot of mine in a moment. And, if it had been directed against another person, Kailas Babu would have understood the joke. But after all that he had heard from his friend, the Government servant, and after all his own exaggerations, a visit from the Lieutenant-Governor seemed the most natural thing in the world. He became very nervous and excited at my news. Each detail of the coming visit exercised him greatly—most of all his own ignorance of English. How on earth was that difficulty to be met? I told him there was no difficulty at all; it was an aristocratic foible not to know English; besides, the Lieutenant-Governor always brought an interpreter with him, and he had expressly mentioned that this visit was to be private.

About midday, when most of our neighbours were at work, and the rest were asleep, a carriage and pair stopped before the lodging of Kailas Babu. Two flunkeys in livery came up the stairs, and announced in a loud voice: 'The Chota Lât Sahib!' Kailas Babu was ready, waiting for him, in his old-fashioned ceremonial robes and ancestral turban, with Ganesh by his side, dressed for the occasion in his master's best clothes.

When the Chota Lât Sahib was announced, Kailas Babu ran panting, puffing and trembling to the door, and led in with repeated salaams, a friend of mine, in disguise. As he did so, he bowed low at each step and walked backwards as well as he could. He had spread his old family shawl over a hard wooden chair on which he asked the Lât Sahib to be seated. He then made a high-flown speech in Urdu, the ancient court language of the Sahibs, and presented on the golden salver a string of gold *mohurs*, the last relics of his broken fortune. The old family servant Ganesh, with an expression of awe bordering on terror, stood behind with the scent-sprinkler, simply drenching the Lât Sahib, and touching him gingerly from time to time with the otto-of-roses from the filigree box.

Kailas Babu repeatedly expressed his regret at not being able to receive His Honour Bahadur with all the ancestral magnificence of his family estate at Nayanjore. There he could have welcomed him with due ceremonial. But in Calcutta, he said, he was a mere stranger and sojourner—in fact, a fish out of water.

My friend, with his tall silk hat on, very gravely nodded. I need hardly say that according to English custom the hat ought to have been removed inside the room. But my friend dared not take it off for fear of detection; and Kailas and his old servant Ganesh were sublimely unconscious of this breach of etiquette.

After a ten minutes' interview, which on his part consisted chiefly of nodding the head, my friend rose to depart. The two flunkeys in livery, as had been planned beforehand, carried off in state the string of gold *mohurs,* the gold salver, the gold ancestral shawl, the silver scent-sprinkler, and the otto-of-roses filigree box; they placed them ceremoniously in the carriage. Kailas Babu regarded this as the usual habit of Chota Lât Sahibs.

I was watching all the while from the next room. My sides were aching with suppressed laughter. When I could hold myself in no longer, I rushed into a room further off, suddenly to discover, in a corner, a young girl sobbing as though her heart would break. When she heard my uproarious laughter, she stood tense in passion, flashing the lightning of her big dark eyes in mine and said with a tearchoked voice: 'Tell me! What harm has my grandfather done to you! Why have you come to deceive him? Why have you come here? Why—'

She could say no more. She covered her face with her hands and broke into sobs.

My laughter stopped instantly. It had never occurred to me that there was anything but a supremely funny joke in this act of mine, and here I discovered that I had given the cruellest pain to this tender little heart. All the ugliness of my cruelty rose up to condemn me. I slunk out of the room in silence, like a whipped dog.

Hitherto I had only looked upon Kusum, the grand-daughter of Kailas Babu, as a somewhat worthless commodity in the marriage market, waiting in vain to attract a husband. But now I found, with surprise, that in the corner of that room a human heart was beating.

The whole night through I had very little sleep. My mind was in a tumult. Very early next morning, I took all those stolen goods back to Kailas Babu's lodgings, to hand them over in secret to the servant Ganesh. I waited outside the door, and, finding no one, went upstairs to Kailas Babu's room. I heard from the passage Kusum asking her grandfather in the most winning voice: 'Dada dearest, do tell me all that the Chota Lât Sahib said to you yesterday. Don't leave out a single word. I am dying to hear it all over again.'

And Dada needed no encouragement. His face beamed with pride as he related all the compliments that the Lât Sahib had been good enough to utter concerning the ancient families of Nayanjore. The girl was seated before him looking up into his face, and listening with rapt attention. She was determined, out of love for the old man, to play her part so well as to allow no suspicion to enter his mind.

My heart was deeply touched, and tears came to my eyes. I stood there in silence in the passage, while Thakur Dada finished his account, with embellishments, of the Chota Lât Sahib's wonderful visit. When at last, he left the room, I took the stolen goods, laid them at the feet of the girl and came away without a word.

Later in the day I called again to see him. According to our ugly modern custom, I had been in the habit of making no greeting at all to this old man when I came into the room. But today I made a low bow and touched his feet. I am convinced the old man thought that the coming of the Chota Lât Sahib to his house was the cause of my new politeness. He was very much gratified by it, and benign serenity shone from his eyes. His friends had looked in, and he had already begun to tell again at full length the story of the Lieutenant-governor's visit with still further adornments of a most fantastic kind. The story of the interview was already becoming epic, both in quality and in length.

When the other visitors had taken their leave, I humbly made my proposal to the old man. I told him that, 'though I could never for a moment hope to be worthy of being received into such an illustrious family in marriage, yet...etc. etc.'

When I made my proposal clear, the old man embraced me and broke out in an excess of joy: 'I am a poor man, and could never have expected such great good fortune.'

That was the first and last time in his life that Kailas Babu confessed his poverty. It was also the first and last time in his life that he forgot, if only for a single moment, the ancestral dignity of the Babus of Nayanjore.

9

The Castaway

As evening drew on, the storm rose to its height. From the terrific downpour of rain, the crash of thunder, and the repeated flashes of lightning, you might think that a battle of gods and demons was raging in the skies. Black clouds waved like the flags of Doom. The Ganges was lashed into fury, and the trees in the gardens on either bank swayed from side to side, sighing and groaning.

In a closed room of one of the riverside houses at Chandernagore, a husband and wife were seated on a bed spread on the floor, discussing intently an important question. Beside them an earthen lamp burned.

The husband, Sharat, was young: 'I wish you would stay a few more days; you would then be able to return home quite strong again.'

The wife, Kiran, was saying: 'I have quite recovered already. It will not, cannot possibly, do me any harm to go home now.'

Every married person will at once understand that the conversation was not quite so brief as I have reported it. The matter was not difficult, but the arguments for and against did not advance it towards a conclusion. Like a rudderless boat, the discussion kept turning round and round the same point: and at last it threatened to be overwhelmed in a food of tears.

Sharat said: 'The doctor thinks you should stop here a few days longer.'

Kiran replied. 'Your doctor knows everything!'

'Well,' said Sharat, 'you know that just now all kinds of sickness are abroad. You would do well to stop here a month or two more.'

'And I suppose at this moment everyone here is perfectly well!'

What had happened was this: Kiran was universal favourite with her family and neighbours, so that, when she fell seriously ill, they were all very anxious about her. The village wiseacres thought it shameless for her husband to make so much fuss about a mere wife and for him even to suggest a change of air. They asked Sharat whether he supposed that no woman had ever been ill before, or whether he had found out that the folk of the place to which he meant to take her were immortal. Did he imagine that the writ of Fate did not run there? But Sharat and his mother turned a deaf ear to them, thinking that the little life of their darling was of greater importance than the united wisdom of a village. People are wont to reason thus when danger threatens their loved ones. So Sharat went to Chandernagore, and Kiran recovered, though she was still very weak. There was a pinched look on her face which filled the beholder with pity, and it wrung his heart to think how narrowly she had escaped death.

Kiran was fond of society and amusement; the loneliness of her riverside villa did not suit her at all.

There was nothing to do, there were no interesting neighbours, and she hated to be busy all day with medicine and diet. There was no fun measuring doses and making fomentations. Such was the subject discussed in their closed room this stormy evening.

So long as Kiran deigned to argue, there was a chance of a fair fight. When she ceased to reply, and with a toss of her head disconsolately looked the other way, the poor man was disarmed. He was on the point of surrendering unconditionally, when a servant called out a message through the closed door.

Sharat got up and on opening the door learnt that a boat had been upset in the storm, and that one of the occupants, a young Brahmin boy and succeeded in swimming ashore at their garden steps.

Kiran was at once her own sweet self and set to work to get out some dry clothes for the boy. She then warmed a cup of milk and invited him to her room.

The boy had long curly hair, big expressive eyes, and as yet no sign of hair on his face. Kiran, after getting him to drink some milk, asked him all about himself.

He told her that his name was Nilkanta, and that he belonged to a theatrical company. They were coming to play in a neighbouring villa, when the boat had suddenly foundered in the storm. He had no idea what had become of his companions. He was a good swimmer and had just managed to reach the bank.

The boy stayed with them. His narrow escape from a terrible death made Kiran take a warm interest in him. Sharat thought the boy's arrival at this moment rather a good thing, as his wife would now have something to amuse her, and might be persuaded to stay for some time longer. Her mother-in-law, too, was pleased at the prospect of benefiting their Brahmin guest by her kindness. And Nilkanta himself was delighted at this double escape from his master and from the other world, as well as at finding a home in this wealthy family.

But very soon Sharat and his mother changed their opinion, and longed for his departure. The boy found a secret pleasure in smoking Sharat's hookahs; he would calmly go off in pouring rain with Sharat's best silk umbrella for a stroll through the village, and make friends with all he met. Moreover, he had adopted a mongrel cur which he petted so recklessly that it came indoors with muddy paws, and left tokens of its visit on Sharat's spotless bed. Then he gathered about him a devoted band of boys of all sorts and sizes, and the result was that not a single mango in the neighbourhood had a chance of ripening that season.

There is no doubt that Kiran had a hand in spoiling the boy. Sharat often warned her about it, but she would not listen to him. She made a dandy of him with Sharat's cast-off clothes, and also gave him new ones. And because she felt drawn towards him, and was curious to know more about him, she was constantly calling him to her own room. After her bath and midday meal, Kiran would seat herself on the bedstead with her betel-leaf box by her side; and while her maid combed and dried her hair, Nilkanta would stand in front and recite pieces out of his repertory with appropriate gesture and song, his elf-locks waving wildly. Thus the long afternoon hours passed merrily away. Kiran would often try to persuade Sharat to sit with her as one of the audience, but Sharat, who had taken a cordial dislike to the boy, refused; nor could Nilkanta play his part half so well when Sharat was there. His mother would sometimes be lured by the hope of hearing sacred names in the recitation; but the love of her midday sleep speedily overcame devotion, and she lay wrapped in dreams.

The boy often had his ears boxed and pulled by Sharat, but as this was nothing to what he had been used to as a member of the troupe, he did not mind it in the least. In his short experience of the world he had come to the conclusion that, as the earth consisted of land and water, so human life was made up of eatings and beatings. And that the beatings largely predominated.

It was hard to tell Nilkanta's age. If it was about fourteen or fifteen, then his face was too old for his years; if seventeen or eighteen, then it was too young. He had either become a man too early or had remained a boy too long. The fact was that, joining the theatrical band when very young, he had played the parts of Radhika, Damayanti, and Sita, and a thoughtful Providence had so arranged things that he grew to the exact stature that his manager required and then growth ceased.

Since everyone saw how small Nilkanta was, and since he himself felt small, he did not receive the respect due to his years. Causes, natural and artificial, combined to make him sometimes seem immature

for seventeen years, and at other times appear a mere lad of fourteen—
but a lad far too knowing even for seventeen. And as no sign of hair
appeared on his face, the confusion became greater. Either because he
smoked or because he used language beyond his years, his lips puck-
ered into lines that showed him to be old and hard; but innocence and
youth shone in his large eyes. I fancy that his heart remained young,
but the hot glare of publicity had been a forcing-house that ripened
untimely his outward aspect.

In the quiet shelter of Sharat's house and garden at Chandernagore, Nature had leisure to work her way unimpeded. Nilkanta had
lingered in a kind of unnatural youth, but now he silently and swiftly
developed beyond that stage. His seventeen or eighteen years were
fully revealed. No one observed the change, and its first sign was this,
that when Kiran treated him like a boy, he felt ashamed. When she one
day gaily proposed that he should play the part of lady's companion,
the idea of dressing as a woman hurt him, though he could not say
why. So now, when she called for him to act over again his old charac-
ters, he disappeared.

It never occurred to Nilkanta that he was even now not much
more than a lad-of-all-work in a strolling company. He even made up
his mind to pick up a little education from Sharat's agent. But, because
Nilkanta was the pet of his master's wife, the agent could not endure
the sight of him. In addition, his restless training made it impossible
for him to keep his mind long engaged; sooner or later, the alphabet
seemed to dance a misty dance before his eyes. He would sit for hours
with an open book on his lap, leaning against a *champak* bush beside
the Ganges. Below, the waves sighed, boats floated past, above his head
birds flitted and twittered restlessly. What thoughts passed through his
mind as he looked down on that book he alone knew, if indeed he did
know. He never advanced from one word to another, but the glorious
thought, that he was actually reading a book, filled his soul with exul-
tation. Whenever a boat went by, he lifted his book, and pretended to
be reading hard, shouting at the top of his voice. But his fit of energy
passed off as soon as the audience was gone.

Formerly he sang his songs automatically but now their tunes
stirred in his mind. Their words were of little import and full of trifling
alliteration. Even the feeble meaning they had was beyond his compre-
hension; yet when he sang—

> *Twice-born bird! Ah! Wherefore stirred*
> *To wrong our royal lady?*
> *Goose, ah, say why wilt thou slay*
> *Her in forest shady?*

he felt transported to another world and to far different folk. This
familiar earth and his own poor life became music, and he was trans-
formed. That tale of the goose and the king's daughter flung upon the
mirror of his mind a picture of surpassing beauty. It is impossible to
say what he imagined himself to be, but the destitute little slave of the
theatrical company faded from his memory.

When at even-tide the child of want lies down, dirty and hungry,
in his squalid home, and hears of prince and princess and fabled gold,
then in the dark hovel lighted by its dim flickering candle, his mind
springs free from its bonds of poverty and misery and walks in fresh
beauty and glowing raiment, strong beyond all fear of hindrance,
through that fairy realm where all is possible.

In this way also, this drudge of wandering players fashioned
himself and his world anew, as he moved in spirit amid his songs. The
lapping water, rustling leaves, and calling birds; the goddess who had
given shelter to him, helpless and forsaken of God; her gracious, lovely
face, her exquisite arms with their shining bangles, her rosy feet as
flower-petals—all these by some mâgic became one with the music of
his song. When the singing ended, the mirage faded, and the Nilkanta
of the stage appeared again, with his wild elf-locks. Then Sharat fresh
from the complaints of his neighbours, the owner of the despoiled
mango-orchard, would come and box his ears and cuff him. The boy
Nilkanta, the leader astray of adoring youth, went forth once more, to
make ever new mischief by land and water and in the branches that are
above the earth.

Shortly after the advent of Nilkanta, Sharat's younger brother, Satish, came to spend his college vacation with them. Kiran was hugely pleased at finding fresh occupation. She and Satish were of the same age, and the time passed pleasantly in games and quarrels and reconciliations and laughter and even tears. She would suddenly clasp him over the eyes from behind with vermillion-stained hands, or she would write 'monkey' on his back, or else she would bolt the door on him from the outside amidst peals of laughter. Satish in his turn did not take things lying down. He would steal her keys and rings, he would put pepper among her betel, he would tie her to the bed when she was not looking.

Meanwhile, heaven only knows what possessed poor Nilkanta. He was suddenly filled with a bitterness which he felt must be avenged on somebody or something. He thrashed his devoted boy-followers for no fault of theirs, and sent them away crying. He would kick his pet mongrel till it made the skies resound with its whinings. When he went out for a walk, he would litter his path with twigs and leaves beaten from the road-side shrubs with his cane.

Kiran liked to see people enjoying good fare. Nilkanta had an immense capacity for eating, and never refused a good thing, however frequently it might be offered. So Kiran liked to send for him to have his meals in her presence, and ply him with delicacies, happy in the bliss of seeing this Brahmin boy eat his fill. But when Satish joined them, she had much less spare time on her hands and was seldom present to see Nilkanta's meals served. Before, her absence made no difference to the boy's appetite, and he would note rise till he had drained his cup of milk and rinsed it thoroughly with water.

But now, if Kiran was not there to ask him to try this and that, he was miserable, and nothing tasted right. He would get up, without eating much, and say to the serving-maid with tears in his voice: 'I am not hungry.' He thought that the news of his repeated refusal, 'I am not hungry,' would reach Kiran; he pictured her concern, and hoped that she would send for him and press him to eat. But nothing of the sort happened. Kiran never knew and never sent for him; and the maid finished whatever he left. He would then put out the lamp in his room, throw himself on his bed in the darkness, and bury his head in the pillow in a paroxysm of weeping. What was his grievance? Against whom? And from whom did he expect redress? At last, when no one else came, Mother Sleep soothed with her soft caresses the wounded heart of the motherless lad.

Nilkanta came to the unshakable conviction that Satish was poisoning Kiran's mind against him. If Kiran was absent-minded and had not her usual smile, he would jump to the conclusion that some trick of Satish had made her angry. He took to praying to the gods, with all the fervour of his hate, to make him at the next rebirth Satish, and Satish him. He had an idea that a Brahmin's wrath could never be in vain; and the more he tried to consume Satish with the fire of his curses, the more did his own heart burn within him. And, upstairs, he would hear Satish laughing and joking with his sister-in-law.

Nilkanta never dared to show his enmity to Satish openly. But he would contrive a hundred petty ways of causing him annoyance. When Satish went for a swim in the river and left his soap on the steps of the bathing-place, he would find on coming back for it that it had gone. Once he found his favourite striped tunic floating past him on the water, and thought it had been blown away by the wind.

One day Kiran wished to entertain Satish, so she sent for Nilkanta to recite as usual, but he stood there in gloomy silence. In great surprise, Kiran asked him what was the matter. But he would not answer. And when again pressed by her to repeat some favourite piece of hers, he answered 'I don't remember it,' and walked away.

At last, the time came for their return home. Everybody was busy packing up. Satish was going with them. But to Nilkanta no one said a word. The question whether he was to go or not seemed to be nobody's concern.

The subject, as a matter of fact, had been raised by Kiran, who had proposed to take him with them. But her husband and his mother and brother had all objected so strenuously that she had let the matter drop. A couple of days before they were to start, she sent for the boy, and with kind words advised him to go back to his home.

He had felt neglected for so long that this touch of kindness was too much for him; he burst into tears. Kiran's eyes were also brimming over. She was filled with remorse at the thought that she had created a tie of affection, which had to be broken.

But Satish was greatly annoyed at the blubbering of this overgrown boy. 'Why does the fool stand there howling instead of speaking?' said he. When Kiran scolded him for an unfeeling creature, he replied: 'My dear sister, you do not understand. You are too good and trustful. This fellow turns up from the Lord knows where, and is treated like a king. Naturally the tiger has no wish to become a mouse again. And he has evidently discovered that there is nothing like a tear or two to soften your heart.'

Nilkanta hurriedly left them. He felt that he would like to be a knife to cut Satish to pieces; a needle to pierce him through and through; a fire to burn him to ashes. But Satish was not even scared. It was only his own heart that bled and bled.

Satish had brought with him from Calcutta a very fine inkstand. The inkpot was set in a mother-of-pearl boat drawn by a German-silver goose supporting a pen-holder. It was a great favourite of his, and he cleaned it carefully every day with an old silk handkerchief. Kiran would laugh, and tapping the silver bird's beak would say—

> *Twice-born bird, ah! Wherefore stirred*
> *To wrong our royal lady?*

and the usual war of words would break out between her and her brother-in-law.

The day before they were to start, the inkstand was missing and was to be found nowhere. Kiran smiled, and said: 'Brother-in-law, your goose has flown off to look for your Damayanti.'

But Satish was in a great rage. He was certain that Nilkanta had stolen it—for several people said they had seen him prowling round the room the night before. He had the accused brought before him, in Kiran's presence. 'You have stolen my inkstand, you thief!' he burst out, 'bring it back at once.' Nilkanta had always taken punishment from Sharat, deserved or undeserved, with perfect equanimity. But, when he was called a thief before Kiran, his eyes blazed with fierce anger, his breast swelled and his throat choked. If Satish had said another word, he would have flown at him like a wild cat and used his nails like claws.

Kiran was greatly distressed at the scene, and taking the boy into another room said in her sweet, kind way: 'Nilu, if you really have taken that inkstand, give it to me quickly, and I shall see that no one says another word to you about it.' Big tears coursed down the boy's cheeks, till at last he hid his face in his hands, and wept bitterly. Kiran came back from the room and said: 'I am sure Nilkanta has not taken the inkstand.' Sharat and Satish were equally positive that no other than Nilkanta could have done it.

But Kiran steadily refused to believe it.

Sharat wanted to cross-examine the boy, but his wife would not allow it.

Then Satish suggested that his room and box should be searched. But Kiran said: 'If you dare do such a thing, I will never forgive you. You shall not spy on the poor innocent boy.' And as she spoke, her wonderful eyes filled with tears. That settled the matter and effectually prevented any further molestation of Nilkanta.

Kiran's heart overflowed with pity at this attempted outrage on a homeless lad. She got two new suits of clothes and a pair of shoes, and with these and a currency note in her hand, she went quietly into Nilkanta's room in the evening. She intended to put these parting presents into his box as a surprise. The box itself had been her gift.

From her bunch of keys she selected one that fitted and noiselessly opened the box. It was so jumbled up with odds and ends that the new clothes would not go in. So she thought she had better take everything out and pack the box for him. At first knives, tops, kite-flying reels, bamboo twigs, polished shells for peeling green mangoes, bottoms of broken tumblers and such things as appeal to a boy's heart were discovered. Then there came a layer of linen, clean and otherwise. And from under the linen there emerged the missing inkstand, goose and all.

Kiran, with flushed face, sat down helplessly with the inkstand in her hand, puzzled and wondering.

In the meantime, unknown to Kiran, Nilkanta had come into the room from behind. He had seen the whole thing and thought that Kiran had come like a thief to catch him in his thieving—and that his crime was discovered. How could he ever hope to convince her that he was not a thief, and that only revenge had prompted him to take the inkstand, which he meant to throw into the river at the first opportunity? In a weak moment he had put it in his box instead. 'I am not a thief,' his heart cried out, 'not a thief!' Then what was he? What could he say? That he had stolen, and that he was still not a thief? He could never explain to Kiran how grievously wrong she was. And then, how could he bear the thought that she had tried to spy on him?

At last, Kiran with a deep sigh replaced the inkstand in the box, and, as if she were the thief herself, covered it up with the linen and the trinkets as she had found them; and at the top she placed the presents, together with the currency note which she had brought for him.

Next day the boy was nowhere to be found. The villagers had not seen him; the police could discover no trace of him. Said Sharat: 'Now, as a matter of curiosity, let us have a look at his box.' But Kiran was obstinate in her refusal to allow such a thing.

She had the box brought up to her own room; and taking out the inkstand, she threw it into the river.

The whole family went home. In a day the garden became desolate. And only that starving mongrel of Nilkanta's remained prowling along the river-banks, whining and whining as if its heart would break.

10

The Son of Rashmani

—: 1 :—

𝒦alipada's mother was Rashmani, but she had to do the duty of the father as well, because when both of the parents have too motherly a feeling, then it is bad for the child. Bhavani, her husband, was wholly incapable of keeping children under discipline. To know why he was bent on spoiling his son, you must hear something of the former history of the family.

Bhavani was born in the famous house of Saniari. His father, Abhaya Charan, had a son, Shyama Charan, by his first wife. When he married again after her death, he had himself passed the marriageable age, and his new father-in-law took advantage of the weakness of his position to have a special portion of the family estate settled on his daughter. In this way he was satisfied that proper provision had been made, in case his daughter should become a young widow. She would be independent of the charity of Shyama Charan.

The first part of his anticipation came true. For very soon after the birth of a son, who was named Bhavani, Abhaya Charan died. It gave the father of the widow great peace and consolation, as he looked forward to his own death, to know that this daughter was properly looked after.

When Bhavani was born, Shyama Charan was quite grown up. In fact his own eldest boy was a year older than Bhavani. He brought up the latter with his own son. In doing this, he never took a farthing from the property allotted to his stepmother, and every year he obtained a receipt from her after submitting detailed accounts. His honesty in this affair surprised the neighbourhood. In fact, they thought that he was a fool to be so honest. They did not like the idea of a division being made in the hitherto undivided ancestral property. If Shyama Charan in some underhand manner had been able to annul the dowry, his neighbours would have admired his sagacity; and there were plenty of people ready to give both advice and material aid in the attainment of such an object. But Shyama Charan, in spite of the risk of crippling his patrimony, strictly set aside the portion allotted to his step-mother and the widow, Vraja Sundari, being by nature affectionate and trustful, trusted Shyama Charan as if he had been her own son. More than once had she chided him for being so particular about her portion of the property. She would tell him that, as she was not going to take her property with her when she died, and as it would in any case revert to the family, it was not necessary to be so very strict in rendering accounts. But he never listened to her.

Shyama Charan was a severe disciplinarian by habit, and his children were perfectly aware of the fact. But Bhavani had every possible freedom, and this gave rise to the impression that he was too partial to his step-brother. But Bhavani's education was sadly neglected and he completely relied on Shyama Charan for the management of his share of the property. He merely had to sign occasional documents without ever giving a thought to their contents. On the other hand, Tarapada, the eldest son of Shyama Charan, was quite an expert in the management of the estate, for he had to act as assistant to his father.

After the death of Shyama Charan, Tarapada said to Bhavani: 'Uncle, we must not live together as we have done for so long, because some trifling misunderstanding might come at any moment and cause a complete break between us.'

Bhavani never imagined, even in his dreams, that a day might come when he would have to manage his own affairs. The world in which he had been born and bred ever appeared to him complete and entire in itself. It was an incomprehensible calamity to him that there could be a dividing line somewhere and that this world of his could be split in two. When he found that Tarapada was immovable and indifferent to the grief and dishonour that such a step would bring to the family, he began to rack his brains to find out how the property could be divided with the least possible disturbance.

Tarapada was surprised at his uncle's anxiety and said that there was no need to trouble about the matter because the division had already been made in the life-time of his grandfather. In amazement, Bhavani exclaimed: 'But I know nothing of this!' Tarapada replied: 'Then you must be the only one in the whole neighbourhood who does not. For, lest there should be ruinous litigation after his death, my grandfather had already given a portion of the property to your mother.' Bhavani thought this not unlikely and asked: 'What about the house?' Tarapada said: 'If you wish, you can keep this house yourself and we shall be contented with the other house in the district town.'

As Bhavani had never been in this town-house, he had neither knowledge of it, nor affection for it. He was astounded at the magnanimity of Tarapada in so easily relinquishing his right to the house in the village where they had been brought up. But when Bhavani told everything to his mother, she struck her forehead with her hand and exclaimed: 'This is preposterous! What I got from my husband was my own dowry and the income from it is very small. I do not see why you should be deprived of your share in your father's property.'

Bhavani said: 'Tarapada is quite positive that his grandfather never gave us anything except this land.'

Vraja Sundari was astonished at this piece of information and informed her son that her husband had made two copies of his will, one of which was still lying in her own box. The box was opened but it was found that there was only the deed of gift for the property belonging to the mother and nothing else. The copy of the will had been taken out.

In their difficulty, they sought advice, and the man who came to their rescue was Bagala, the son of their family *guru*. The father had charge of the spiritual needs of the village; the material side was left to the son. The two of them had as it were divided between themselves the next world and this. Whatever might be the result for others, they themselves had nothing to complain of from this division. Bagala said that, if the will was missing, the ancestral property must be equally divided between the brothers.

Just as this time, a copy of a will appeared supporting the claims of the other side. In this document there was no mention of Bhavani and the whole property was given to the grandsons at the time when no son was born to Bhavani. With Bagala at the helm Bhavani set out on his voyage across the perilous sea of litigation. When his vessel at last reached harbour, his funds were nearly exhausted and the ancestral property was in the hands of the opposite party. The land which was given to his mother had dwindled to such an extent, that it could barely shelter them, much less keep up the family dignity. Then Tarapada went away to the district town and they never met again.

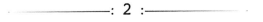

: 2 :

This act of treachery pierced the heart of the widow like an assassin's knife. To the end of her life, almost daily she would heave a sigh and say that God would never suffer such injustice. She was quite firm in her faith when she said to Bhavani: 'I do not know your law or your law courts, but I am certain that my husband's true will and testament will some day be recovered. You will find it again.'

Bhavani was so helpless in worldly matters that assurances such as these gave him great consolation. He settled down in his inactivity, certain in his own mind that his pious mother's prophecy was bound to be fulfilled. After his mother's death, his faith became all the stronger, since the memory of her piety became more radiant through death's mystery. He never felt the stress of their poverty which as the years went by became more and more acute. The obtaining of the necessaries of life and the maintenance of family traditions—those seemed to him like play-acting on a temporary stage, not real things. When the expensive clothing of his earlier days was worn out and he had to buy cheaper materials, it merely amused him. He smiled and said to himself—'These people do not know that this is only a passing phase of my future. Their surprise will be all the greater, when some day I shall celebrate the Puja festival with a magnificence they never dreamt of.'

This certainty of future prodigality was so clear to his mind's eye that present penury escaped his attention. His servant, Noto, was the principal companion with whom he discussed these things. They used to have animated conversations, in which sometimes the servant's opinion differed from the master's as to the propriety of bringing down a theatrical troupe from Calcutta for these future occasions. Frequently Bhavani would reprimand Noto for his natural miserliness in these items of future expenditure.

Bhavani's one anxiety, the absence of an heir to inherit his vast possible wealth, was dissipated by the birth of his son. The horoscope plainly indicated that the lost property would come back to this boy.

From this time onwards, Bhavani's attitude was changed. It became cruelly difficult for him now to bear his poverty with his old amused equanimity, because he felt that he had a duty towards this new representative of the illustrious house of Saniari, whose future was destined to be so glorious. That the traditional extravagance could not be indulged in on the occasion of the birth of his child gave him the keenest sorrow. He felt as if he were cheating his own son. To compensate for this he spoiled the boy inordinately with an inordinate amount of spoiling.

Bhavani's wife Rashmani, had a different temperament from her husband. She never felt any anxiety about keeping up the family tradition of the Chowdhuris of Saniari. Bhavani was quite aware of the fact and smiled indulgently to himself, as though nothing better could be expected from a woman who came from a Vaishnava family of very humble lineage. Rashmani frankly acknowledged that she could not share the family sentiments; what concerned her most was the welfare of her child.

There was hardly an acquaintance in the neighbourhood with whom Bhavani did not discuss the question of the lost will; but he never spoke a word about it to his wife. Once or twice he had tried, but her perfect unconcern had made him drop the subject. She neither paid attention to the past greatness of the family, nor to its future glories—she kept her mind busy with the actual needs of the present, and those needs were not small.

When the Goddess of Fortune deserts a house, she usually leaves some of her burdens behind, and this ancient family was still encumbered with its host of dependants, though its own shelter was nearly crumbling to dust. These parasites take it as an insult if they are asked to do anything in return. Their heads ache at the mere smell of kitchen smoke. They are afflicted with sudden rheumatism the moment they are asked to run as errand. Therefore all the responsibilities of maintaining the family were laid upon Rashmani herself. Women lose their delicacy and refinement, when they are compelled night and day to haggle with their destiny over things pitifully small, and for this they are blamed by those whom their toil supports.

Besides her household affairs Rashmani had to keep all the accounts of the little landed property which remained and also to make arrangements for collecting the rents. Never before was the estate managed with such strictness. Bhavani had been quite incapable of collecting his dues: Rashmani never made any remission of the least fraction of rent. The tenants, and even her own agents, reviled her behind her back for the meanness of the family from which

she came. Even her husband occasionally used to protest against her
harsh economy which was contrary to the practice of the world-famed
house of Saniari.

Rashmani quite ungrudgingly took all the blame upon herself and
openly confessed the poverty of her parents. Tying the end of her *sari*
tightly round her waist, she went on with her household duties in her
own vigorous fashion and made herself thoroughly disagreeable, both
to the inmates of the house and to her neighbours. But nobody ever
had the courage to interfere. Only one thing she carefully avoided. She
never asked her husband to help her in any work and she was nerv-
ously afraid of his taking any responsibility. Indeed she was always
strenuously engaged in keeping her husband idle; and as he had
received the best possible training in this direction, her object was
completely fulfilled.

Rashmani was middle-aged before her son came. Before this all the
pent-up tenderness of the mother in her and all the love of the wife
had their centre of devotion in her simple-hearted, good-for-nothing
husband. Bhavani was merely an overgrown child. This was the reason
why, after the death of her husband's mother, she had to assume the
position of mother and master in one.

In order to protect her husband from the invasions of Bagala, the
son of the *guru*, and other calamities, Rashmani adopted such a stern
demeanour, that her husband's companions used to be terribly afraid
of her. She never had the opportunity, which a woman usually has, of
keeping her fierceness hidden and of softening the keen edge of her
words, or of maintaining that dignified reserve towards men which is
proper for a woman.

Bhavani meekly accepted his wife's authority with regard to
himself, but it became extremely hard for him to obey her in matters
that concerned Kalipada, his son. The reason was, that Rashmani never
regarded Bhavani's son from the point of view of Bhavani himself. In
her heart she pitied her husband and said: 'Poor man, it was his misfor-
tune, not his fault, to be born into a rich family.' That is why she never
could expect her husband to deprive himself of any of his accustomed
comforts. Whatever might be the condition of the household finances,

she tried hard to keep him in the ease and luxury he was accustomed to. Under the regime all expense was strictly limited except in the case of Bhavani. She would never allow him to notice if there was something unavoidably missing in his meals, or if his clothes wore out without her being able to replace them. She would blame some imaginary dog for spoiling dishes that were never made and would blame herself for her carelessness. She would attack Noto for letting some garments be stolen or lost. This had the usual effect of rousing Bhavani's sympathy on behalf of his favourite servant and he would try to defend him. Indeed it often happened that Bhavani confessed with bare-faced shamelessness that he had used some article that had never been bought, and for whose loss Noto was blamed; but had not the power to invent the conclusion of the story and was obliged to rely upon the fertile imagination of his wife who was also the accuser!

Although Rashmani treated her husband in this way, she acted very differently towards her son. For he was her own child and why should he be allowed to give himself airs? Kalipada had to be content with a few handfuls of puffed rice and some treacle for his breakfast. During the cold weather he had to wrap his body as well as his head with a thick rough cotton *chaddar*. She would call his teacher before her and warn him never to spare her boy, if he were the least neglectful with his lessons. This treatment of his own son was the hardest blow that Bhavani Charan had suffered during the days of his destitution. But as he had always acknowledged defeat at the hands of the powerful, he had not the spirit to stand up against his wife in her method of bringing the boy up.

The clothes which Rashmani provided for her son, during the Puja festivities, were made of such poor material that in former days the very servants of the house would have rebelled if such had been offered to them. But Rashmani more than once tried her best to explain to her husband that Kalipada, being the most recent addition to the Chowdhury family, had never known their former splendour and so would be quite glad to get what was given to him. But this pathetic ignorance of the boy concerning his own destiny hurt Bhavani more than anything else, and he could not forgive himself for deceiving the child.

Sometimes Kalipada would dance for joy and rush to him to show him some trivial present from his mother, and then Bhavani's heart would suffer torture.

Bagala, the *guru's* son, was now very rich owing to his agency in the lawsuit that had brought about Bhavani's ruin. With the money which he had in hand he used to buy cheap tinsel wares from Calcutta before the Puja holidays. Invisible ink, absurd combinations of stick, fishing rod and umbrella—letter-paper with pictures in the corner—silk fabrics bought at auctions, and other things of this kind, attractive to the simple villagers—these were his stock in trade. All the forward young men of the village vied with one another in rising above their rusticity by purchasing these sweepings of the Calcutta market, which, they were told, were absolutely necessary for the city gentry.

Once Bagala had bought a wonderful toy—a doll dressed as a foreign woman—which, when wound up, would rise from its chair and begin to fan itself with sudden energy. Kalipada was fascinated by it. He had a very good reason to avoid asking his mother about the toy; so he went straight to his father and begged him to buy it for him. Bhavani instantly agreed, but when he heard the price his face fell. Rashmani kept all the money and Bhavani went to her like a timid beggar. He began with all sorts of irrelevant remarks and then took a desperate plunge into the subject with startling incoherence.

Rashmani's only remark was 'Are you mad?' Bhavani Charan sat silent, wondering what to say next.

'Look here,' he exclaimed, 'I don't think I need milk pudding daily with my dinner.'

'Who told you that?' said Rashmani sharply.

'The doctor says it's very bad for biliousness.'

'The doctor's a fool!'

'But I'm sure that rice agrees with me better than your *luchis*. They are so indigestible.'

'I've never seen the least sign of indigestion in you. You have been accustomed to them all your life!'

Bhavani Charan was ready enough to make sacrifices, but in this case he was not allowed to make them. Butter might rise in price, but the number of his *luchis* never decreased. Milk was quite enough for him at his midday meal, but curds had also to be supplied because that was the family tradition. Rashmani could not have borne to see him sit down to a meal, without curds. Therefore, all his attempts to cut down his daily provisions, so that the fanning foreign woman might enter his house, were an utter failure.

Then Bhavani paid an apparently purposeless visit to Bagala, and after a great deal of round-about talk asked about the foreign doll. Of course his straitened circumstances had long been known to Bagala, yet Bhavani was perfectly miserable when he had to think twice about buying this doll for his son. But what could he do with empty pockets? Swallowing his pride, he produced an expensive old Kashmir shawl, and said in a husky voice: 'I am very hard up at present and I haven't got much cash. So I am determined to part with this shawl to buy that doll for Kalipada.'

If the object offered had been less valuable than this Kashmir shawl, Bagala would at once have closed the bargain. But knowing that he could not take possession of this shawl in face of village opinion, and still more in face of Rashmani's watchfulness, he refused to accept it; and Bhavani had to go back disappointed, with the Kashmir shawl under his arm.

Kalipada asked every day for that foreign fanning toy, and Bhavani smiled every day and said—'Wait a bit, my boy, till the seventh day of the moon comes.' But every day it became more and more difficult to keep up that smile.

On the fourth day of the moon, Bhavani suddenly made up his mind to broach the subject to his wife, and said:

'I've noticed that there's something wrong with Kalipada—he is not looking well.'

'Nonsense,' said Rashmani, 'he's in the best of health.'

'Haven't you noticed him sitting silent for hours together?'

'I should be very greatly relieved if he could sit still for as many minutes.'

When all his sorrows had missed their mark, and no impression had been made, Bhavani Charan heaved a deep sigh and, passing his fingers through his hair, went away and sat down on the verandah and began to smoke with fearful vigour.

On the fifth day, at his breakfast, Bhavani refused the curds and the milk pudding without touching them. In the evening, he only took a single piece of *sandesh*. The *luchis* were left unheeded. He complained of want of appetite. This time a considerable breach was made in the fortifications.

On the sixth day, Rashmani took Kalipada into the room and calling him by his pet name, said, 'Betu, you are old enough to know that it is the half-way house to stealing, to desire what you can't have.'

Kalipada whimpered and said: 'What is that to me? Father promised to give me that doll.'

Rashmani tried to explain to him how much lay behind his father's promise—how much pain, how much affection, how much loss and privation. Rashmani had never in her life talked thus to Kalipada, because it was her habit to give short and sharp commands. It filled the boy with amazement when he found his mother coaxing him and explaining things at such length, and child though he was, he could fathom something of the deep suffering of his mother's heart. Yet at the same time, it will be easily understood that it was hard for him to turn his mind away altogether from that captivating foreign fanning woman. He pulled a long face and began to scratch the ground with his foot.

This hardened Rashmani's heart at once, and she said severely: 'Yes, you may weep and cry, or be angry but you shall never get what I do not mean you to have.' And she hastened away without another word.

Kalipada went out, and Bhavani Charan who was still smoking his hookah noticed him from a distance. So he got up and walked in the opposite direction as if he had some urgent business. Kalipada ran to him and said, 'But what about that doll?' Bhavani could not raise a smile that day. He put his arm round Kalipada's neck and said:

'Babu, wait a little. I have some pressing business to get through. Let me finish it first, and then we will talk about it.' Saying this, he went out of the house.

Kalipada saw him brush a tear from his eyes. He stood at the door and watched his father, and it was quite apparent, even to him, that he was going nowhere in particular, and that he was dragging with him the weight of a hopeless despair.

Kalipada at once went back to his mother and said, 'Mother, I don't want that foreign doll.'

That morning Bhavani Charan returned late. When he sat down to eat, after his bath, it was evident by the look on his face, that the curds and the milk pudding would fare no better with him than on the day before, and that the best part of the fish would go to the cat.

Just at this moment, Rashmani brought in a cardboard box, tied up with string, and set it before her husband. Her intention had been to reveal the mystery of this packet to him, when he went to take a nap after his meal. But in order that the curds and the milk and the fish might not again be neglected, she had to disclose its contents before she had intended. So the foreign doll came out of the box, and without more ado began to fan itself vigorously.

And so the cat had to go away disappointed. Bhavani remarked to his wife that the cooking was the best he had ever tasted. The fish soup was incomparable, the curds had set with a firmness that was rarely attained and the milk pudding was superb.

On the seventh day of the moon, Kalipada got the toy for which he had been pining. During the whole of that day, he allowed the foreigner to go on fanning herself, and thereby made his boy companions jealous. In any other case, this performance would have seemed to him monotonous and tiresome, but knowing that on the following day he would have to give the toy back, his constancy to it on that single occasion was unabated. At a fee of two rupees per diem Rashmani had hired it from Bagala.

On the eighth day of the moon, Kalipada heaved a deep sigh and returned the toy, along with the box and twine, to Bagala. From that day forward, Kalipada began to share the confidences of his mother, and it became so absurdly easy for Bhavani to give expensive presents every year, that it surprised even himself.

When, with the help of his mother, Kalipada came to know that nothing in this world would be gained without paying for it with the inevitable price of suffering, his character rapidly matured and he became a valued assistant to his mother in her daily tasks. It came to be the natural rule of life with him, that no one should add to the burden of the world, but that each should try to lighten it.

When Kalipada won a scholarship at the Vernacular Examination, Bhavani proposed that he should give up his studies and take in hand the supervision of the estate. Kalipada went to his mother and said: 'I shall never be a man, if I do not complete my education.'

His mother said: 'You are right, Baba, you must go to Calcutta.'

Kalipada explained to her, that it would not be necessary to spend a single pice on him; his scholarship would be sufficient, and he would try to get some work to supplement it.

But it was necessary to convince Bhavani of the wisdom of the course. Rashmani did not wish to employ the argument that there was very little of the estate remaining to require supervision, for she knew how it would hurt him. She said that Kalipada must become a man whom everyone could respect. But all the members of the Chowdhury family had attained their respectability without ever going a step outside the limits of Saniari. The outer world was as unknown to them as the world beyond the grave. Bhavani, therefore, could not conceive how anybody could think of a boy like Kalipada going to Calcutta. But the cleverest man in the village, Bagala, fortunately agreed with Rashmani.

'It is perfectly clear,' he said, 'that one day Kalipada will become a lawyer; and then he will set matters right concerning the property of which the family has been deprived.'

This was a great consolation to Bhavani Charan, and he brought out the file of records concerning the stolen will and tried to explain the whole thing to Kalipada by daily discussion. But his son had no proper enthusiasm and merely echoed his father's sentiment about the solemn wrong.

The day before Kalipada left for Calcutta, Rashmani hung round his neck an amulet containing mantras to protect him from all evils. She gave him at the same time a fifty-rupee note, advising him to keep it for any special emergency. This note, the symbol of his mother's numberless daily acts of self-denial, was the truest amulet of all for Kalipada. He determined to keep it by him and never to spend it, whatever might happen.

—————: 3 :———

From this time onward, Bhavani indulged less and less in the old interminable discussions about the theft of the will. His one topic of conversation was the marvellous adventure of Kalipada in search of education. Kalipada was actually engaged in his studies in the city of Calcutta! Kalipada knew Calcutta as well as the palm of his hand! Kalipada had been the first to hear the great news that another bridge was going to be built over the Ganges near Hooghly! The day on which the father received his son's regular letter, he used to go to every house in the village to read it to his neighbours, and he could scarcely find time even to take his spectacles from his nose. On arriving at each house, he would remove them from their case with the utmost deliberation; then he would wipe them carefully with the end of his *dhoti,* then, word by word, he would slowly read the letter through to one neighbour after another with something like the following comment:

'Brother, just listen! What *is* the world coming to? Even dogs and the jackals are to cross the holy Ganges without washing the dust from their feet! Who could imagine such sacrilege?'

No doubt it was very deplorable; but all the same it gave Bhavani Charan a peculiar pleasure to communicate at first hand such important news from his son's letter, and this more than compensated for the spiritual disaster which must surely overtake the numberless creatures of this present age. To everyone he met, he solemnly nodded his head and prophesied, that the days were soon coming when Mother Ganges would disappear altogether; all the while cherishing the hope, that the news of such a momentous event—when it happened—would come to him, by letter from his son.

Kalipada, with very great difficulty scraped together just enough money to pay his expenses till he passed the Matriculation Examination and again he won a scholarship. Bhavani at once made up his mind to invite all the village to a feast, for he imagined that his son's good ship of fortune had now reached its haven, and that there would be no more need for economy. But he received no encouragement from Rashmani.

Kalipada was fortunate enough to secure a corner in a students' lodging-house near his college. The proprietor allowed him to occupy a small room on the ground-floor, which was absolutely useless for other lodgers. In exchange for this and his board, he had to coach the son of the owner of the house. The one great advantage was that there would be no chance of any fellow-lodger ever sharing his quarters. So, although the place was badly ventilated, his studies were uninterrupted.

Those of the students who paid their rent and lived in the upper storey had no concern with Kalipada; but soon it became painfully evident that those who live up above have the power to hurl missiles at those below with the more deadly force because of their height. The leader of those above was Sailen.

Sailen was the scion of a rich family. It was unnecessary for him to live in students' mess, but he successfully convinced his guardians that this would be best for his studies. The real reason was that Sailen was naturally fond of company, and the students' lodging-house was an ideal place where he could have all the pleasure of companionship without any of its responsibilities. It was the firm conviction of Sailen that he was a good fellow and a man of feeling. The advantage of harbouring such a conviction was that it needed no proof in practice. Vanity, unlike a horse or an elephant, requires no expensive fodder.

Nevertheless, as Sailen had plenty of money, he did not allow his vanity merely to graze at large; he took special pride in keeping it stall-fed. It must be said to his credit that he had a genuine desire to help people in their need; but the desire in him was of such a character, that if a man in difficulty refused to come to him for help, he would turn round on him and do his best to add to his trouble. His mess-mates had their tickets for the theatre bought for them by Sailen, and it cost them nothing to have occasional feasts. They could borrow money from him with no intention of paying it back. When a newly married youth was in doubt about the choice of some gift for his wife, he could fully rely on Sailen's good taste. On these occasions, the love-lorn youth would take Sailen to the shop and pretend to select the cheapest and least suitable presents: then Sailen with a contemptuous laugh would intervene and select the right thing. At the mention of the price, the young husband would pull a long face, but Sailen would always be ready to abide by his own superior choice and to pay for it.

In this manner, Sailen became the acknowledged patron of the students upstairs. It made him intolerant of the insolence of anyone who refused to accept his help. Indeed, to help others in this way had become his hobby.

Kalipada, in his tattered jersey, used to sit on a dirty mat in his damp room below and recite his lessons, swinging himself from side to side to the rhythm of the sentence. It was a sheer necessity for him to get that scholarship next year.

Kalipada's mother had made him promise, before he left home for Calcutta, that he would avoid the company of rich young men. He, therefore, bore the burden of his indigence alone, strictly keeping himself from those who had been more favoured by fortune. But to Sailen, it seemed a sheer impertinence that a student as poor as Kalipada should yet have the pride to avoid his patronage. Besides this, in his food and dress and everything, Kalipada's poverty was so blatantly exposed, it hurt Sailen's sense of decency. Every time he looked down into Kalipada's room, he was offended by the sight of the cheap clothing, the dingy mosquito net and the tattered bedding. Whenever he passed on his way to his own room in the upper storey, he could not avoid the sight of these things. To crown it all, there was that absurd amulet which Kalipada always had hanging round his neck, and those daily rites of devotion which were so ridiculously out of fashion!

One day Sailen and his followers condescended to invite Kalipada to a feast, thinking that his gratitude would know no bounds. But Kalipada sent an answer saying that his habits were not the same as theirs and it would not be good for him to accept the invitation. Sailen was unaccustomed to such a refusal, and it roused in him all the ferocity of his insulted benevolence. For some days after this, the noise in the upper storey became so loudly insistent that, Kalipada, try as he might, could not go on with his studies. He was compelled to spend the greater part of his days studying in the park, and to get up very early and sit down to his work long before it was light.

Owing to his half-starved condition, his mental overwork, and his badly-ventilated room, Kalipada began to suffer from continual headaches. There were times when he was obliged to lie on his bed for three or four days together. But he made no mention of his illness in his letters to his father. Bhavani himself was certain that, just as vegetation grew rank in his village surroundings, so comforts of all kinds sprang up of themselves from the soil of Calcutta. Kalipada never for a moment disabused his mind of that misconception. He did not fail to write to his father, even when suffering from one of these sharp attacks of pain. The deliberate rowdiness of the students in the upper storey at such times added to his distress.

Kalipada tried to make himself as unobtrusive as possible, in order to avoid notice; but this did not bring him relief. One day, he found that a cheap shoe of his own had been taken away, and replaced by one of an expensive foreign make. It was impossible for him to go to college in such an incongruous pair. He made no complaint, however, but bought some old second-hand shoes from the cobbler. One day, a student from the upper storey came into his room and asked him:

'Have you, by any mistake, taken away my silver cigarette case?'

Kalipada was very annoyed and answered:

'I have never been inside your room.'

The student stooped down. 'Hullo!' he said, 'here it is!' And he picked up a valuable cigarette case from the corner of the room.

Kalipada determined to leave this lodging-house as soon as ever he had passed the Intermediate Examination, provided he could only get a scholarship to enable him to do so.

Every year the students of the house used to celebrate the Saraswati Puja. Though the greater part of the expenses were borne by Sailen, everyone else contributed according to his means. The year before, they had contemptuously left out Kalipada from the list of contributors, but this year, merely to tease him, they came with their subscription book. Kalipada instantly paid five rupees to the fund, though he had no intention of participation in the feast. His penury had long brought on him the contempt of his fellow-lodgers, but this unexpected gift of five rupees became to them insufferable. The Saraswati Puja was performed with great magnificence and the five rupees could easily have been spared. It had been hard indeed for Kalipada to part with such a sum. While he ate the food given him in his landlord's house he had no control over the time at which it was served. Besides this, since the servants brought him the food, he did not like to criticise the dishes. He preferred to provide himself with some extras; and after the forced extravagance of his five-rupee subscription, he had to forego all this and suffer in consequence. His headaches became more frequent, and though he passed his examination, he failed to obtain the scholarship that he desired.

The loss of the scholarship drove Kalipada to do extra work as a private tutor, and would not allow him to change his unhealthy room in the lodging-house. The students overhead had hoped that they would be relieved of his presence, but punctually to the day, the room on the lower floor was unlocked. Kalipada entered, clad in the same old dirty check Parsee coat. A coolie from Sealdah Station took down from his head a steel trunk and other miscellaneous packages, and laid them on the floor of the room; and a long wrangle ensued as to the proper amount due to the coolie.

In the depths of those packages, there were mango chutnies and other condiments which his mother had specially prepared. Kalipada was aware that, in his absence, the upper-storey students, on mischief bent, would not scruple to come by stealth into his room. He was especially anxious to keep these home gifts from their cruel scrutiny. As tokens of home affection they were supremely precious to him; but to the town students they denoted merely the boorishness of poverty-stricken villagers. The earthen vessels were crude, and were covered by earthen lids fixed on with flour-paste. They were neither glass nor porcelain and were therefore sure to be regarded with insolent disdain by rich town-bred people.

Formerly Kalipada used to keep these stores hidden under his bed, covering them up with old newspapers. But this time he took the precaution of always locking the door, even if he went out for a few minutes. This still further roused the spleen of Sailen and his party. It seemed to them preposterous that the room, which was poor enough to draw tears from the eyes of the most hardened burglar, should be as carefully guarded as if it were a second Bank of Bengal.

'Does he actually believe,' they said among themselves, 'that the temptation will be irresistible for us to steal that Parsee coat?'

Sailen had never visited this dark and mildewed room from which the plaster was dropping. The glimpses that he had obtained, while going upstairs—especially when, in the evening, Kalipada, the upper part of his body bare, would sit poring over his books with a smoky lamp beside him—were, he felt, enough to choke him. Sailen asked his boon companions to explore the room below, and find out the treasure which Kalipada had hidden. Everybody felt greatly amused at the proposal.

The lock on Kalipada's door was a cheap one, any key would fit. One evening, when Kalipada had gone out to his private work, two or three of the students with an exuberant sense of humour took a lantern, unlocked the room and entered. It did not need a moment's search to discover the pots of chutney under the bed, but these hardly seemed valuable enough to demand such watchful care on the part of Kalipada. Further search disclosed a key on a ring under the pillow. They opened the steel trunk with the key and found a few soiled clothes, books and writing material. They were about to shut the box in disgust when they saw, at the very bottom, a packet covered by a dirty hand-kerchief. On uncovering three or four wrappers, they found a currency note for fifty rupees. This made them burst into peals of laughter. They felt certain that Kalipada suspected the whole world, because of this fifty-rupee note!

The meanness of this suspicious precaution deepened the intensity of their contempt for Kalipada. At that moment, they heard a footstep outside. They hastily shut the box, locked the door, and ran upstairs with the note in their possession.

Sailen was vastly amused. Though fifty rupees was a mere trifle, he could never have believed that Kalipada had so much money in his trunk. They all decided to watch the result of this loss upon the queer creature downstairs.

When Kalipada came home that night after his work was over, he was too tired to notice any disorder in his room. One of his worst attacks of nervous headache was coming on, and he went straight to bed.

The next day, when he brought out his trunk from under the bed to take out his clothes, he found it open. He was naturally careful, but it was not unlikely, he thought, that he had forgotten to lock it the day before.

But when he lifted the lid he found all the contents topsy-turvy, and his heart gave a great thud when he discovered that the note, given to him by his mother, was missing. He searched the box over and over again in the vain hope of finding it, and when he had made certain of his loss, he flung himself upon his bed and lay like and dead.

Just then, he heard footsteps on the stairs and every now and then an outburst of laughter from the upper room. It struck him that this was not an ordinary theft: Sailen and his party must have taken the note to amuse themselves and make a jest of it. It would have given him less pain if a thief had stolen it. It seemed to him that these young men had laid their impious hands upon his mother herself.

Then, for the first time, Kalipada ascended those stairs. He ran to the upper floor—the old jersey on his shoulders—his face flushed with anger and with the pain of his illness. As it was Sunday, Sailen and his company were seated in the verandah, laughing and talking. Without any warning, Kalipada burst upon them and shouted:

'Give me back my note!'

If he had begged it of them, they would have relented; but the sight of his anger made them furious. They started up from their chairs and exclaimed:

'What do you mean, sir? What do you mean? What note?'

Kalipada shouted: 'The note you have taken from my box!'

'How dare you?' they shouted back. 'Do you take us for thieves?'

If Kalipada had had any weapon in his hand at that moment, he certainly would have killed one of them. But just as he was about to spring, they fell on him, and four or five of them dragged him down to his room and thrust him inside.

Sailen said to his companions. 'Here take this hundred-rupee note, and throw it to that *dog!*'

They all loudly exclaimed: 'No! Let him climb down first and give us a written apology. Then we shall consider it!'

Sailen's party all went to bed at the proper time and slept the sleep of the innocent. In the morning they had almost forgotten Kalipada. But some of them passing his room, heard the sound of talking and they thought that possibly he was deep in consultation with some lawyer. The door was shut from the inside. They tried to overhear, but what they heard had nothing legal about it. It was quite incoherent.

They informed Sailen. He came down and stood with his ear close to the door. The only thing that could be distinctly heard was the word 'Father.' This frightened Sailen. He thought that possibly Kalipada had gone mad with grief through the loss of that fifty-rupee note. Sailen shouted, 'Kalipada Babu!' two or three times, but got no answer. Only the muttering continued. Sailen called: 'Kalipada Babu—please open the door. Your note has been found.' But still the door was not opened, and the muttering went on.

Sailen had never anticipated such a result as this. He did not express a word of repentance to his followers, but he felt the sting of repentance all the same. Some advised him to break open the door, others thought that the police should be called in—for Kalipada might be in a dangerous state of lunacy. Sailen at once sent for a doctor who lived close at hand. When they burst open the door, they found the bedding hanging from the bed and Kalipada lying on the floor unconscious. He was tossing about and throwing up his arms and muttering, with his eyes red and open and his face flushed. The doctor examined him and asked whether there were any relatives near at hand; for the case was serious.

Sailen answered that he knew nothing, but would make inquiries. The doctor then advised the removal of the patient at once to an upper room where he could be nursed properly day and night. Sailen took him up to his own room and dismissed his followers. He got some ice and putting it on Kalipada's head began to fan him. Kalipada, fearing that mocking references would be made, had with special care concealed the names and address of his parents from these people. So Sailen had no alternative but to open his box. He found two bundles of letters tied up with ribbon. One of them contained his mother's letters: the other contained his father's. His mother's letters were the fewer in number. Sailen closed the door and began to read them. He was startled when he saw the address,—Saniari, the house of the Chowdhuris—and then the name of the father, Bhavani. He folded up the letters, and sat still, gazing at Kalipada's face. Some of his friends had casually mentioned that there was a resemblance between Kalipada and himself. But he had been offended at the remark and did not believe it. Today he discovered the truth. He knew his own grandfather, Shyama Charan, had a step-brother named Bhavani; but the latter history of the family had remained a secret to him. He did not even know that Bhavani had a son, named Kalipada; and he never suspected that Bhavani had come to such an abject state of poverty as this. He now felt not only relieved, but proud of his relative, Kalipada, who had refused to become one of his protégés.

———: 4 :———

Knowing that his party had insulted Kalipada almost every day, Sailen was reluctant to keep him in the lodging-house with them. So he took another more suitable house and kept him there. Bhavani started in haste for Calcutta the moment he received a letter from Sailen inform-ing him of his son's illness. Rashmani parted with all her savings, and told her husband to spare no expense. It was not considered proper for the daughters of the great Chowdhury family to leave their home and go to Calcutta, unless absolutely obliged, and therefore she had to remain behind offering prayers to all the tutelary gods. When Bhavani Charan arrived, he found Kalipada still unconscious and delirious. It nearly broke Bhavani's heart, when he heard himself called 'Master Mashai'. Kalipada often called him in his delirium and Bhavani tried to get his son to recognise him, but in vain.

The doctor came again and said the fever was abating. He thought the case was taking a more favourable turn. As for Bhavani he could not imagine that his son was past recovery. He *must* live: it was his destiny to live. Bhavani was much struck with the behaviour of Sailen. It was difficult to believe that he was not of their own kith and kin. He supposed all this kindness to be due to the town training which Sailen had received. Bhavani spoke to Sailen disparagingly of the country habits of village people like himself.

Gradually the fever went down and Kalipada recovered conscious-ness. He was astonished beyond measure when he saw his father sitting in the room beside him. His first anxiety was lest he should discover the miserable state in which he had been living. But what would be harder still to bear was, that his father with his rustic manners might become the butt of the people upstairs. He looked round, but could not recognise his own room and wondered whether he had been dreaming. But he found himself too weak to think.

He supposed that it was his father that had removed him to this better lodging, but he could not calculate how he could possibly bear the expense. The only thing that concerned him at that moment was that he felt he must live and for that he had a claim upon the world.

Once, when Bhavani was absent, Sailen came in with a plate of grapes in his hand. Kalipada could not understand this at all, and wondered if there was some practical joke behind. He became excited at once and wondered how he could save his father from annoyance. Sailen set the plate down on the table and humbly touching Kalipada's feet said: 'My offence has been great; pray forgive me.'

Kalipada started and sat up on his bed. He could see that Sailen's repentance was sincere and he was greatly moved.

When Kalipada first came to the students' lodging-house, he had felt strongly drawn towards this handsome youth. He never missed a chance of looking at his face, when Sailen passed his room on his way upstairs. He would have given all the world to be friends with him, but the barrier was too great to be broken down. Now, today, when Sailen brought him the grapes and asked his forgiveness, he silently looked into his face and accepted the grapes as a token of his repentance.

It amused Kalipada greatly when he noticed the intimacy that had sprung up between his father and Sailen. Sailen used to call Bhavani Charan 'grandfather' and exercised to the full the grandchild's privilege of joking with him. The principal object of the jokes was the absent 'grandmother'. Sailen confessed that he had taken the opportunity of Kalipada's illness to steal all the delicious chutnys which his 'grand-mother' had made with her own hand. The news of his act of 'thieving' gave Kalipada very great joy. He found it easy to deprive himself, if he could find anyone who could appreciate the good things made by his mother. Thus, the time of his convalescence became the happiest period in Kalipada's life.

There was only one flaw in this ideal happiness. Kalipada had a fierce pride in his poverty, which prevented him from speaking about his family's better days. Therefore, when his father used to talk of his former prosperity, Kalipada winced. Bhavani could not keep to himself the one great event of his life—the theft of that will, which he was absolutely certain he would some day recover. Kalipada had always regarded this as a kind of mania of his father's and in collusion with his mother, he had often humoured him concerning this amiable weakness. But he shrank in shame when his father talked about it to Sailen.

He noticed particularly that Sailen did not relish such conversation and that he often tried with a certain amount of feeling to prove its absurdity. But Bhavani, who was ready to give in to others in matters much more serious, in this matter was adamant. Kalipada tried to pacify him by saying that there was no great need to worry about it, because those who were enjoying the benefit were almost the same as his own children, since they were his nephews.

Sailen could not bear such talk for long and he used to leave the room. This pained Kalipada, because he thought that Sailen might get quite a wrong conception of his father and imagine him to be a grasping worldly old man. Sailen would have revealed his own relationship to Kalipada and his father long before this, but this talk about the theft of the will prevented him. It was hard for him to believe that his grandfather or father had stolen the will; on the other hand, he could not but think that some cruel injustice had been done in depriving Bhavani of his share of the ancestral property. Therefore, he gave up arguing when the subject was brought forward and took the first possible opportunity to leave.

Though Kalipada still had headaches in the evening, with a slight rise in temperature, he did not take it at all seriously. He became anxious to resume his studies, because he felt it would be a calamity to him if he again failed to obtain a scholarship. He secretly began to read once more, without taking any notice of the strict orders of the doctor. Kalipada asked his father to return home, assuring him that he was in the best of health. Bhavani had been all his life fed and nourished and looked after by his wife; he was pining to get back. He did not therefore wait to be pressed.

On the morning of his intended departure, when he went to say goodbye to Kalipada, he found him very ill indeed, his face flushed with fever and his whole body burning. He had been committing to memory page after page of his text-book of Logic half through the night, and for the remainder he could not sleep at all. The doctor took Sailen aside. 'This relapse,' he said, 'is fatal.' Sailen came to Bhavani and said: 'Kalipada requires a mother's nursing: she must be brought to Calcutta.'

It was evening when Rashmani came, and she only saw her son alive for a few hours. Not knowing how her husband could survive such a terrible shock she altogether suppressed her own sorrow. Her son was merged in her husband again, and she took up this burden of the dead and the living on her own aching heart. She said to her God, 'It is too much for me to bear.' But she did bear it.

It was midnight. Wearied out by grief, Rashmani had fallen asleep soon after reaching her home in the village. But Bhavani had no sleep that night. Tossing on his bed for hours he would heave a deep sigh saying—'Merciful God!' Then he got up from his bed and went out. He entered the room where Kalipada used to learn his lessons as a child. The lamp shook as he held it in his hand. On the wooden settee there was still the torn, ink-stained quilt, made long ago by Rashmani herself. On the wall were figures in Euclid and symbols in Algebra drawn in charcoal. The remains of a *Royal Reader No. III* and a few exercise books were lying about; and the one odd slipper of his infancy, which had evaded notice so long, kept its place in the dusty obscurity of the corner of the room. Today it had become so important that nothing in the world, however great, could keep it hidden any longer. Bhavani put the lamp in its niche, and silently sat on the settee, his eyes were dry, and his throat choking.

Bhavani opened the shutters on the eastern side and stood still, grasping the iron bars, gazing into the darkness. Through the drizzling rain he could see the outline of the clump of trees at the end of the outer wall. At this spot Kalipada had made his own garden. The passion flowers which he had planted had grown thick and dense. While he gazed at this, Bhavani felt choking with sorrow. There was nobody now to wait for and expect daily. The summer vacation had come, but no one would come back home to fill the vacant room and use its old familiar furniture.

'O my darling,' he cried, 'my darling son.'

He sat down. The rain came faster. A sound of footsteps was heard among the grass and withered leaves. Bhavani's heart stood still. He hoped it was…that which was beyond any hope. He thought it was Kalipada himself come to see his own garden—and in his downpour of rain how wet he would be! Anxiety about this made him restless. Then somebody stood for a moment in front of the iron window bars. The cloak round his head made it impossible for Bhavani to see his face clearly; he was of the same height as Kalipada.

'My boy!' cried Bhavani, 'You have come!' and he hurried to open the door.

But when he came to the spot where the figure had stood, there was no one to be seen. He walked up and down in the garden through the drenching rain, but no one was there. He stood still for a moment raising his voice and calling—'Kalipada,'—but no answer came. The servant, Noto, who was sleeping in the cowshed, heard his cry and came out and coaxed him back to his room.

Next morning, Noto, while sweeping the room found a bundle just underneath the grated window. He brought it to Bhavani, who opened it and found it was an old document. He put on his spectacles and after reading a few lines rushed into Rashmani's room and gave the paper into her hand.

'What is it?' Rashmani asked.

'It is the will!' replied Bhavani.

'Who gave it to you?'

'He himself came last night to give it to me.'

'What are you going to do with it?'

Bhavani said: 'I have no need of it now.' And he tore the will to pieces.

When the news reached the village, Bagala proudly nodded his head and said: 'Didn't I prophesy that the will would be recovered through Kalipada?'

But the grocer Ramcharan replied: 'Last night when the ten o'clock train reached the station, a handsome-looking young man came to my shop and asked the way to the Chowdhurys' house, and I thought he had some sort of bundle in his hand.'

'Absurd,' said Bagala.

OTHER HARDBACK BOOKS

» 1984 by George Orwell
   Fiction/Classics, ISBN: 9788193545836

» Abraham Lincoln by Lord Charnwood
   Biography/Leaders, ISBN: 9789387669147

» Alice's Adventures in Wonderland by Lewis Carroll
   Children's/Classics, ISBN: 9789387669055

» Animal Farm by George Orwell
   Fiction/Classics, ISBN: 9789387669062

» Gitanjali by Rabindranath Tagore
   Fiction/Poetry, ISBN: 9789387669079

» Great Speeches of Abraham Lincoln by Abraham Lincoln
   History/General, ISBN: 9789387669154

» How to Stop Worrying and Start Living by Dale Carnegie
   Self-Help/General, ISBN: 9789387669161

» How to Win Friends and Influence People by Dale Carnegie
   Self-Help/Success, ISBN: 9789387669178

» Illust. Biography of William Shakespeare by Manju Gupta
   Biography/Authors, ISBN: 9789387669246

» Madhubala by Manju Gupta
   Biography/Actors, ISBN: 9789387669253

» Mansarover 1 (Hindi) by Premchand
   Fiction/Short Stories, ISBN: 9789387669086

» Mansarover 2 (Hindi) by Premchand
   Fiction/Short Stories, ISBN: 9789387669093

» Mein Kampf (My Struggle) by Adolf Hitler
   Biography/Leaders, ISBN: 9789387669260

» My Experiments with Truth by Mahatma Gandhi
   Biography/Leaders, ISBN: 9789387669277

» Relativity by Albert Einstein
   Sciences/Physics, ISBN: 9789387669185

OTHER HARDBACK BOOKS

» Selected Stories of Tagore by Rabindranath Tagore
  Fiction/Short Stories, ISBN: 9789387669307

» Sense and Sensibility by Jane Austen
  Fiction/Classics, ISBN: 9789387669109

» Siddhartha by Hermann Hesse
  Fiction/Classics, ISBN: 9789387669116

» Tales from India by Rudyard Kipling
  Fiction/Short Stories, ISBN: 9789387669123

» Tales from Shakespeare by Charles & Mary Lamb
  Children's/Classics, ISBN: 9789387669314

» The Art of War by Sun Tzu
  Self-Help/Success, ISBN: 9789387669321

» The Autobiography of a Yogi by Paramahansa Yogananda
  Biography/General, ISBN: 9789387669192

» The Diary of a Young Girl by Anne Frank
  Biography/General, ISBN: 9789387669208

» The Jungle Book by Rudyard Kipling
  Children's/Classics, ISBN: 9789387669338

» The Light of Asia by Sir Edwin Arnold
  Religion/Buddhism, ISBN: 9789387669130

» The Miracles of Your Mind by Joseph Murphy
  Self-Help/Success, ISBN: 9789387669215

» The Origin of Species by Charles Darwin
  Sciences/Life Sciences, ISBN: 9789387669345

» The Power of Your Subconscious Mind by Joseph Murphy
  Self-Help/General, ISBN: 9789387669222

» The Science of Getting Rich by Wallace D. Wattles
  Self-Help/Success, ISBN: 9789387669239

» Think and Grow Rich by Napoleon Hill
  Self-Help/Success, ISBN: 9789387669352